Sir Walter Scott

A Tour in the Highlands in 1803

A Series of Letters, Addressed to Sir Walter Scott

Sir Walter Scott

A Tour in the Highlands in 1803
A Series of Letters, Addressed to Sir Walter Scott

ISBN/EAN: 9783744764186

Printed in Europe, USA, Canada, Australia, Japan

Cover: Foto ©Andreas Hilbeck / pixelio.de

More available books at **www.hansebooks.com**

A TOUR IN THE HIGHLANDS.

A TOUR IN THE HIGHLANDS

IN 1803:

A Series of Letters

BY

JAMES HOGG, THE ETTRICK SHEPHERD,

ADDRESSED TO

SIR WALTER SCOTT, Bart.

Reprinted from 'The Scottish Review.'

ALEXANDER GARDNER,
PAISLEY; AND PATERNOSTER ROW, LONDON.

1888.

INTRODUCTORY NOTE.

The following letters, descriptive of a tour which the Ettrick Shepherd made in the Highlands in the year 1803 have recently been discovered by his daughter, Mrs. Garden, among her father's papers. They were to all appearance intended for the eye of Sir Walter Scott, but whether they were ever read by him is unknown. So far as can be ascertained after the most careful search they have never before been published. There is no reference to them in Hogg's Autobiography, and until recently the survivors of his family were not aware of their existence. The letters speak for themselves, and it is unnecessary here to say more than that they appear to have been written by the Shepherd from memory soon after his return home, and some five years before the publication of *The Lady of the Lake.*

A TOUR IN THE HIGHLANDS

In 1803.

———————

DEAR SIR,—As you were, or pretended to be, much diverted with my whimsical account of a journey which I made through the North Highlands last year, you will not be displeased at hearing that I am just now returned from a long circuit through the Western Highlands and Isles, of which I also intend giving you an account by letters. But in the meantime I promise, nay I swear, that I will endeavour, by making no digressions, and curtailing my remarks, to confine this correspondence within more circumscribed bounds than that of last year, of which I now proceed to give you an instance.

On the twenty-seventh of May I again dressed myself in black, put one shirt, and two neckcloths in my pocket; took a staff in my hand, and a shepherd's plaid about me, and left Ettrick on foot, with a view of traversing the West Highlands, at least as far as the Isle of Skye. I took the road by Peebles for Edinburgh, and after being furnished with letters of introduction to such gentlemen as were most likely to furnish me with the intelligence which I wanted respecting the state of the country. I took a passage in the 'Stirling Fly' for that town. I got only a short and superficial view of the old palace of Linlithgow, and satisfied myself with only making my uncle's observation on viewing the Abbey of Melrose; 'Our masons can mak nae sic houses now-a-days.'

I got a deal of information as we passed along from the Rev. Mr. Somerville of Stirling, who was a passenger in the coach, and seemed a very specious, intelligent man. He showed me the Earl of Stair's very extensive plan of the battle of Dettingen, and entertained me with many curious remarks respecting the ancient harbour and town of Camella, the capital of the Picts, situated beyond Linlithgow, as also the most minute and just description of the battles of Falkirk and Bannockburn, all of which I have written in my journal, and as they are much better described elsewhere than I am capable of doing, I entirely decline it, though I wish from my heart that the distinctions of Englishmen and Scot were entirely disannulled and sunk in that of Britons. I will tell you a story which was told by one in the coach.

'A good many years ago a North and South Briton fell into a warm dispute about the privileges resulting to each country from the Union; each of them divesting his own country entirely of any share of them. At length the Scot safely observed, that if the English had no advantage by the Union, why were they so forward in promoting it, and why were the Scots so backward to agree to it?'

'Why sir, as to the former, because it freed them from the devastations committed by their plundering parties. And as to the latter, because it deprived them of the rich booties which they reaved from England at the expiration of every temporary truce.'

'Aye, aye, was that the way? I did not know, I'm unacquainted with history, but what the d——l had the English ado but to wear them back.'

'Why sir, at a fair engagement, in open war they never could stand us; but having their own mountains and forests so near for a safe retreat, it was impossible to prevent their plundering parties from committing frequent depredations.'

'Aye, aye, I did not know these things,' said the Scot, 'and were the English too hard for them at a fair engagement?'

'Indeed sir, they were. The best and bravest of the Scots allowed of that.'

'Aye, aye, I'm unacquainted with history, but it is believed to have been otherwise where I live.'

'Where,' said the Englishman, 'do you live?'

'At Bannockburn!'

'Hem——.'

Not another word ensued. The subject entirely dropped, and the shrewd Caledonian sat squirting in the fire as if he had meant nothing by the answer.'

I lodged on the Castle-hill, in company with a Mr. MacMillan, who came with us in the coach from Edinburgh, and was bound for Lochaber. We arose next morning before the sun, and had a most advantageous and enchanting view of the links of Forth, and the surrounding country, forming altogether a landscape unequalled by any of the same nature in Scotland.

This having been always the principal pass for an army, either to or from the North, hath in consequence been the scene of many bloody encounters. A description of all the battles that have been fought in view of Stirling Castle would furnish matter for volumes. Many of these have been decisive, and settled the fates of thousands, from which dismal circumstance so often occurring, the place in ancient times took the name of Strevlin, or the valley of strife.

We took the road by Doune, and reached Callander of Menteith at eight A.M., where we breakfasted at an inn in company with the laird of Macnab, and after I had furnished myself with some provisions for the day, departed. The management of the land under tillage continued to grow worse, and in the neighbourhood of Callander there were some of it in a very poor and weedy state, which is the more to be regretted as it appears by some fields adjoining that there was the means of enriching it within reach. I did not stay at any of these *towns* to make enquiries into the present state of their population, trade, and manufactures, sufficient to justify an attempt toward a description of them, therefore I will not detain you by a random, or borrowed account of them, but hasten on, lest I break my oath at the very first.

At Kilmahog, a paltry village about a mile beyond Callander, I parted with MacMillan, and crossing the Teith, turning to the left. You may guess that I was glad at getting safely past this village, for its name signifies *the burial place of Hogg*. It is pleasantly situated on the north-east bank of the river, and is intersected by a dam, over which have been erected several buildings. I proceeded several miles without meeting with any thing remarkable. I went quite out of my road to see Glenfinlas, merely because it was the scene of a poem in which I delighted, but could see nothing more than in other places. The hills were covered with mist down to the middle ; yet I saw enough to convince me that it was an excellent sheep range. Returning, I went by the bridge of Turk, passing a little curiously shaped hill covered with wood, which, with the shores of Loch Venachar, are worthy of going a good way to view even although the Trossachs were not beyond them. But the description of these I must defer until my next, and shall close this as soon as I have reminded you that I have now come above an hundred miles, which would have been four letters at least, last year.

I remain, Sir, your ever faithful

J. H.

DEAR SIR,—As I know that you have seen the Trossachs yourself, and as so many have seen them, and no doubt have described them minutely, I will not attempt a particular description of them, but they are indeed the most confused piece of Nature's workmanship that I ever saw, consisting of a thousand little ragged eminences all overhung with bushes, intersected with interstices, the most intricate and winding imaginable.

On entering among them, surely said I, mentally, Nature hath thrown these together in a rage. But on seeing the spreading bushes overhanging the rocks, and hearing the melody of the birds, I softened the idea into *one of her whims.* But as I had set out with a mind so intent on viewing the scenery of the Highlands, and coming. to such an interesting place on the very first day that I entered them, I was more than ordinarily delighted. It was a little past noon on a Sabbath day when I arrived there. The air was unusually still and dark, not a breath moved the leaves that hung floating over the impending precipices of the Trossachs, nor caused one dark furl on the smooth glassy surface of the winding Loch Katrine. Every species of the winged creation that frequent the woods and mountains of Caledonia, were here joined that day in a grateful hymn in praise of their great Creator. Not one key remained untouched of all the Italian gamut. It was indeed a Dutch concert, where every one sung his own song, from the small whistle of the wren, to the solemn notes of the cuckoo, sounded on an E and C, a double octave lower, and from the sprightly pipe of the thrush and blackbird, to the rough harp of the pye and raven. And that the anthem might be complete, the imperial eagle hovered like a black mote in the skirts of the mist, at whose triumphant yell all the woodland choristers were for some seconds mute ; and like menials in the presence of their lord, began again one after another with seeming fear and caution.

The landscape at large was quite spoiled by a thick, lowering mist, that hid in shades all the high mountains which should have made up the back-ground of this romantic scene. It also confined, and bowed down my contemplations to what most employs them, namely, the things below. These, on such a day, would naturally have arisen, with my eyes, to the tops of the hills, and from thence to heaven, and consequently to Him who made heaven and earth and—the Trossachs. But knowing, notwithstanding of our mental depravity, that clouds and darkness surround Him, and as I was become surrounded with mist, I knew it needless even to attempt it. I had no guide along with me, and it is probable that I might miss some of the most interesting places. I lost myself in the mazes of the river, and for a while believed, what was impossible, namely, that I had got to the other side of the river without perceiving it. The manner in which it works its way amongst the rocks, is not the least striking of the whole. One while it seems quite impeded in its progress, at other times, wheeling and boiling in the most terrific manner, always in ferment, and in a seeming perplexity at what chasm it shall next make its escape by.

I took my dinner, consisting of some biscuits and a cut of cheese, beside a crystal spring at the foot of a rock ; and during my stay there had formed a definite conclusion respecting the formation of the Trossachs. I concluded, that prior to the universal deluge, the Trossachs had formed a steep bar between the two hills, and that the whole of Glen Gyle and Loch Katrine had been one loch, which had formed subterraneous passages among the rocks, to such an extent as had prevented it filling up; but on the declension of the waters of the Flood from around it, unable to sustain the mighty pressure, the Trossachs had given way; when the impetuous torrent had carried all before it saving the everlasting rocks, which yet remain, the shattered monuments of that dreadful breach. This theory is supported by two remaining evidences. First, that the western side of these eminences are all bare and solid rock; while on the opposite sides of the larger ones there are quantities of loose stones and some soil amassed. And second, that the ravines are deeper, and the knolls higher, on, and near, the bottom of the glen, and continue gradually to diminish as you ascend the hills on each side, until they totally disappear. However, my dear sir, I have no hopes that you will treat this probable discovery with a greater share of approbation than you do all my natural and experimental philosophy, namely, by.laughing at it.

I now left the Trossachs, and proceeded up the north side of Loch Katrine, on the shores of which there is still a good proportion of wood, though small in comparison with what it seems once to have been. Many extensive banks that have once been covered with large trees, are only recognizable to have been so by

thousands of decaying stumps.   Even the Trossachs themselves
have suffered severely in wild beauty by the ravages of the axe.
But what they have lost in beauty they have gained in utility.
They are now covered with stocks of tolerably good sheep, and
there is still a sufficiency of wood to serve them for shelter in
winter, which is all that is requisite for the store farmer.   The
lands belong mostly, either to the Hon. Miss Drummond, or the
Earl of Moray, and are generally, though not very large, good
sure farms, and will in time bring large rents.

The inhabitants acknowledge that they do not suffer by snows
lying long in winter, but that, owing to the dryness of their herbage, their flocks are often much reduced in condition during the
spring months, and that when the lambing season commences
with them, many of the lambs are in danger of perishing.

I began now to be afraid that I might be disappointed of a
lodging during the night, there being no public houses in the
bounds.   I went on, however, without asking, until I came to
the house of Glen Gyle.   It was then growing late, and there
was no other human habitation for many miles. I had, twelve
years ago, been sent on an errand to the house of Glen
Gyle, to ask permission of M'Gregor, the laird, to go
through his land with a drove of sheep.   He was then an
old man, and seemed to me to be a very queer man ; but
his lady granted my request without hesitation, and seemed to
me an active, social woman.   Therefore I expected, from the
idea that I had formed of her character, to be very welcome

B

there, and never knew, until I went to the house, that the laird was dead, and the lady and her family removed to the neighbourhood of Callander; while the farm and mansion-house were possessed by two farmers. When I called, one of them came to the door. I asked the favour of a night's lodging; but the important M'Farlane made use of that decisive moment to ask me half a score of questions before he desired me to walk in. I experienced the greatest kindness and attention from all the family when once I got amongst them. M'Alpin, the other farmer, I found to be a very considerable man, both in abilities and influence, but the most warm and violent man in a dispute, though ever so trivial, that ever entered into one. If any one advanced a theory of which he did not approve, he interrupted them with a loud and passionate *hububub*. On the preceding summer five gentlemen from Glasgow were benighted there, and calling at the door, desired M'Alpin to speak with them. He sent word that they might go about their business, for he would be d——d if he held any conversation with a pack of Glasgow weavers.

I remain yours, etc.,

J. H.

———

DEAR SIR,—There is nothing about Glen-Gyle that admits of particular description. It is situated at the head of Loch Katrine, and surrounded by black rocks. It was one of Rob Roy's principal haunts, to whom Glen-Gyle was related.   M'Alpin showed me the island in Loch Katrine where he confined the Marquis of Montrose's steward, after robbing him of his master's rents, and where he had nearly famished him.   The Macgregors have a burial place at Glen-Gyle, surrounded by a high wall. On one of their monuments their coat of arms and motto are engraved.   Query.   Was it not remarkable that both you and I should, each of us have made Glen-Gyle a party in a ballad in imitation of the ancients, and that before we had either seen or heard of each other?   Answer.   The poetical sound of the name, sir.

I now left Glen-Gyle in order to cross the mountains into Glenfalloch.   I did not, however, take the nearest way, but held towards the top of a hill on the left hand, from which I knew there was a charming prospect, with which I had formerly been greatly surprised.   As I hinted above, I had in the summer of 1791 passed through that country with sheep.   On a Saturday night we lay with our sheep in the opening of a wood by the side of Loch Ard, and during the whole of the Sabbath following there was so dark a fog, that we could scarcely see over our drove. Although we got permission, we did not go by Glen-Gyle, but by the garrison of Inversnaid, and the night again overtook us on the top of this hill.   The mist still continued dark, and though my neighbour (companion,) who was a highlandman, knew the road, I was quite unconscious what sort of a country we were in. When I waked next morning the sun was up, and all was clear, the mist being wholly gone. You can better judge of my astonishment than I can express it, as you are well aware what impression such a scene hath on my mind. Indeed it was scarcely possible to have placed me in another situation in Scotland where I could have had a view of as many striking and sublime objects by looking about me. Loch Katrine with its surrounding scenery stretching from one hand; Loch Lomond on the other. The outline of Ben Lomond appeared to particular advantage, as did the cluster of monstrous pyramids on the other side. One hill, in the heights of Strathfillan, called Ben Leo, was belted with snow, and from that direction had a particularly sharp, peaked appearance, being of a prodigious height.

Besides all this I had drank some whisky the preceding evening, and had a very indistinct recollection of our approach to that place, and it was actually a good while ere I was persuaded that every thing I saw was real. I sat about an hour contemplating the different scenes with the greatest pleasure, before I awaked my comrade.

I was very anxious to be on the same spot again, and went out of my way to reach it, expecting to experience the same delightful feelings that I had done formerly. In this, however, I was disappointed, but was not a little surprised on recollecting the extraordinary recurrence of circumstances as to time and place. It was not only the same day of the week but the same day of the same month when I was on the same spot before. The two Sabbaths preceding these two days had been as remarkable for mist and darkness as the days themselves were for clearness and perspicuity of objects. In short, my whimsical fortune seemed endeavouring to make me forget the twelve years that had elapsed. But it would not do.

Musing on these objects I fell into a sound sleep, out of which I was at length awaked by a hideous, yelling noise. I listened for some time before I ventured to look up, and on throwing the plaid off my face, what was it but four huge eagles hovering over me in a circle at a short distance ; and at times joining all their voices in one unconceivable bleat. I desired them to keep at a due distance, like Sundhope's man, for I was not yet dead, which, if I had been, I saw they were resolved that I should not long remain a nuisance amongst the rocks of Glenfalloch.

I now shaped my course towards Kieletur, on the head of the glen, possessed by Mr. Grieve, from the south country, intending to reach Glenorchy that night, for I supposed that I had a cousin, a shepherd, there, whom I had not seen for twelve years, and whom I esteemed very much. But before I reached Kieletur I learned that Mr. Grieve was absent at the fair on Dumbarton Muir, and that my cousin had left Glenorchy, and was gone to a shealing at the back of Ben Vorlich, where he was herding for Mr. Wallace of Inverouglas. I then turned back, took my dinner at the change-house of Glenfalloch, and going through the hills, reached my friend's hut that night.

This Glenfalloch which I now left is the property of Mr. Campbell. It is divided into large farms, and having been long

under sheep the hills are become green, and the stocks very good.
My cousin's cottage was situated by a small lake called Loch
Sloy, in as savage a scene as can be conceived, betwixt the high,
rugged mountains and Ben Vorlich and Ben Vane.   The brows
of each of these were adorned with old wreaths of snow, and
though it was then the month of June so much snow fell during
the night that I was there that the heat of next day did not
nearly dissolve it on the tops of these hills.   He received me with
all the warmth of the most tender friendship, lamenting that he
could so ill accommodate me.   I soon made him easy on that
score, and then he was never satisfied in his enquiries about the
welfare of his dearest relations and friends in Ettrick.   The
family consisted of eleven in all that night, and indeed we were
curiously lodged.   They were but lately come to that place, and
had got no furniture to it; nor indeed was it any wonder, it being
scarcely possible to reach it on foot.   We slept on the same floor
with four or five cows, and as many dogs, the hens preferring the
joists above us.   During the night the cattle broke loose, if they
were at all bound, and came snuffing and smelling about our
couch, which terrified me exceedingly, there being no rampart
nor partition to guard us from their inroads.   At length I heard,
by the growling of the dogs, that they were growing jealous of
them.   This induced me to give them the hint, which they were
not backward in taking, for they immediately attacked their
horned adversaries with great spirit and vociferation, obliging
them to make a sudden retreat to their stalls, and so proud were

the staunch curs of this victory gained in defence of their masters, that they kept them at bay for the rest of the night. Had it not been for this experiment, they could scarcely have missed tramping to death some of the children, who were lying scattered on the floor.   Add to all this confusion, that there was an old woman taken very ill before day.   We were afraid of immediate death, and Walter Bigger, the other shepherd, manifested great concern, as not knowing how it was possible to get her to a Christian burial-place.   She actually died next week, and I think they would be obliged to bury her where they were.

Now sir; mark this situation, and join me in admiring my whimsical fortune, which seems to take a pleasure in reverses, by thus carrying me out of one extremity into another. I say, mark my company here in this hovel. I was in the midst of dying wives, crying children, pushing cows, and fighting dogs; and the very next day, at the same hour, in the same robes, same body, same spirit, I was in the splendid dining-room in the Castle of Inveraray, surrounded by dukes! lords! ladies! silver, silk, gold, pictures, powdered lacqueys, and the devil knows what!   O Mr. Scott, Mr. Scott, thou wilt put me stark mad some day.

Now I say, was it a light thing?   Was it showing any regard for a poor bard's brains, knowing as you well did, how susceptible his mind is of impressions corresponding with the different images conveyed by his senses, to persuade him to go through the Trossachs, and the Duke of Argyll's bowling-green, than which no scenery can be more creative of ideas, although sublime, yet gloomy and severe; and as a contrast to thrust me all at once, out of these, headlong amidst all the transcendent beauty, elegance, and splendour of Inveraray. Well, you think nothing of this, but if I had lost my judgment, what had you to answer for?

I remain, dear Sir, your most obliged

J. H.

—————

DEAR SIR,—It would be by far too tedious were I to give you a minute detail of all my proceedings about Inveraray, where I was detained four days; yet it would be unpardonable were I to omit describing some of my principal blunders and embarrassments; for every hour during the time that I remained there was marked by one or other of these.

I sent a man from the inn with your letter to Colonel Campbell, who returned his compliments, naming the hour when *he would do himself the pleasure of waiting on me!* Mark that, sir. He was punctual to his time; and immediately took me with him to the Castle. His unaffected simplicity of manners soon rendered me quite easy and happy in his company. He led me through a number of the gayest apartments, and at length told me he was going to introduce me to Lady Charlotte. 'By no means,' said I, 'for heaven's sake. I would be extremely glad could I see her at a little distance, but you need never think that I will go in amongst them.' 'Distance!' exclaimed

he. You shall dine with her to-day and, to-morrow.' So saying he went towards a door. I declare, the idea of being introduced to a lady of whom I had heard so much as a paragon of
beauty, elegance, and refined taste ; and who had been the grace
and envy of Courts, raised in my breast such a flutter, I cannot
tell you how I felt. He then bolted into a small circular room
in one of the turrets, where her ladyship was sitting with some
others, closely engaged in something, but I cannot tell what it
was were I to die for it : and I am vexed to this hour that I had
not noted what they were employed in when alone.

She stood up and received me with the greatest familiarity
and good humour in the world, which she hath entirely at
command ; told me the other ladies' names, and enquired kindly
for you and Mrs. Scott ; then asked some questions about
Ettrick Banks and Yarrow Braes. All which I answered in the
best manner I was able. I saw that by her assumed vivacity she
was endeavouring to make me quite easy ; but it was impossible.
I was struck with a sense of my inferiority, and was quite bam-
boozled. I would never have known that I was so ill had there
not unluckily been a mirror placed up by my leg. Not knowing
very well where to look, I looked into it. Had you seen the
figure I made, you would have behaved just as I did. My upper
lip was curled up, my jaws were fallen down, my cheeks were all
drawn up about my eyes, which made the latter appear very
little, my face was extraordinary red, and my nose seemed a
weight on it. On being caught in this dilemma I really could

c

not contain myself, but burst out a-laughing. The ladies looked at one another, thinking I was laughing at them. However, to bring myself off, I repeated something that the Colonel was saying, and pretended to be laughing at it. I should soon have been as ill as ever I was, had not he relieved me by proposing to withdraw in order to see some paintings which we were talking of. Her ladyship, however, thought proper to accompany us through several apartments, leading her little daughter by the hand, a most beautiful stem of the noble bough.

On coming to the north door of the castle the colonel ordered a man to play upon a pipe which was concealed in a walking cane of his, and which sounded exactly like the bagpipe at a distance. When the duchess came within hearing of the music she danced round, setting to the sweet little child, and when she thought that Jack, as she called him, was too severe in his jokes upon Sir William Hart, she popped his hat over the rail, into the sunk way. I was extremely gratified by this behaviour of her ladyship, it became her so well, and I was certain that it was assumed, merely on account of seeing me at such a loss.

Now you will be expecting that I should still be in a worse condition when first introduced to his Grace the Duke, and indeed I was within a little way of being very ill, but got off better than could have been expected. This plaguey bluntness! shall I never get rid of it? He was much indisposed, and I did not see him all that day, but he sent in his compliments with Colonel Campbell, desiring to see me at dinner with him to-morrow. The first time that we encountered was thus. I was returned from the top of Duniqueich, and just as I reached the castle gate, a coach drove up, out of which an old gentleman with a cocked hat, and a scarlet coat alighted. I thought him some old officer, and mounted the steps without minding him, but meeting on the flags Captain Campbell, with whom I had been in company before, I asked who these were. He said they were the Duke and Doctor Campbell. He was by this time advancing toward me, and I was not knowing how I should address him. But he, who it seems had been enquiring who I was, relieved me by addressing me by name, and welcoming me to Inveraray. I thanked his Grace, and hoped he was got better of his indisposition. He said he was rather poorly yet, and desired me to walk in: adding, 'your friend Colonel Campbell will be here immediately.' I followed his Grace through the dining-room, where he had the condescension to sit down and hold a few minutes tête-a-tête with me. He said I had arrived in a very good season for getting a peaceable and undisturbed view of Inveraray, and asked if I had yet been shown anything that was worthy of notice. I said the Colonel had taken much pains in showing me both the inside of the castle and the policies* around it. 'Then,' said he, smiling, 'I am sure that you have seen more than you are pleased with, and that you are even more pleased than edified.' I assured his Grace that I considered myself not a

---

* Grounds.

little instructed, as well as pleased, by having seen so much that was quite unequalled by anything that I had ever seen before. He at length desired me to amuse myself with these books and charts, for that he must go and dress. I had not sat long when Colonel Campbell entered, who in a little time left me also, on the same pretence, that of *dressing for dinner*. I said he was well enough dressed ; it was a silly thing that they could not put on clothes in the morning that would serve them during the day. He proved that that would never do, and went his way laughing.

It was not long until the Duke rejoined me, all clad in black, as indeed all the gentlemen were who sat at table. I was always in the utmost perplexities, not knowing servants from masters. There were such numbers of them, and so superbly dressed, that I daresay I made my best bow to several of them. I remember in particular of having newly taken my seat at dinner, and observing one behind me I thought he was a gentle-man wanting a seat, and offered him mine.

I was so proud that although I did not know how to apply one third of the things that were at table, unless I called for a thing I would not take it when offered to me. I had called for a shave of beef, and was falling on without minding either gravy, mus-tard, or spice, which were proffered. I refused all. 'What!' said the Colonel, 'L—d do ye eat your beef quite plain?' 'Perfectly plain, sir,' said I, 'saving a little salt, and so would you if you knew how much more wholesome it were.' By great good fortune I was joined by several in this asseveration which my extremity suggested.

The Duke talked freely to me about his farming, and told me he had given orders to Mr. ———, who had the superintendence of all his rural affairs, and who was a very sensible man, and a countryman of my own, to take a ride with me to-morrow and show me his cattle, sheep, etc. This brings me to give you an account of our ride, which I intend to do in my next, passing over everything that occurred in the interim.

I remain, Sir, with the utmost respect, yours,

J. H.

———

DEAR SIR,—You must now suppose me mounted on a fine brown hunting mare, as light as the wind, and as mad as the devil, and Mr. ——— on an excellent grey pony, riding full drive through part of the Duke's land which he occupied himself. We took a view of his breeding cows and some oxen, which were greatly superior to any that I ever saw in beauty and compactness. They are certainly the best breed of Highland cattle produced in Scotland, and indeed they have advantages which it is beyond the power of most men to afford. I have been told that Campbell of Islay, and he only, hath long disputed the field with Argyll for the best breed of Highland cattle, and it is the opinion of some that although the latter frequently outsells the other at the markets, yet it is as much owing to the great distance that the Islay cattle must needs be driven, as to the superiority of the breed.   It is truly amazing the prices that these two houses draw for their cattle, it being much more than double the average price at Dumbarton Market.

The sheep that we saw were partly of the Cheviot, and partly of the Scotch kinds; but both rather of inferior breed. Mr. —— excused this by alleging that the Cheviot breed was but lately introduced, and they had not had time to improve them, and that the other kind was got from some of the Duke's farmers who were removing, and who could not otherwise dispose of them at value.   However it was, they were on excellent pasture that would have produced the best of sheep; and I remarked to Mr. —— that it was a shame to see such a stock upon such land. He was no better pleased with many of my observations, than I was with him in general.

On our return his grace asked me several things, and amongst others, what I thought of Mr. ——.   I said I did not rightly understand him; he was surely the worse of drink. 'That was impossible,' he said, ' at this time of day;' and besides, said he, ' I conversed with him since your return.   He is perfectly sober. You surely must be mistaken about Mr. ——.' ' I certainly am mistaken my lord,' said I, 'for I look on him as the worst specimen of your Grace's possessions that I have seen about all Inveraray.'   Perhaps I said too much, but I could not help telling my mind. Colonel Campbell was like to burst during this dialogue, and indeed, little as he pretended to know about rural economy, I could have gathered more from a three hours' conversation with him, than I could have done with Mr. —— in as many weeks. His whole consisted in boasting.

His Grace had the kindness that day to walk with me up to the workshops where his mechanics were employed, and showed and described to me, several specimens of curious implements in husbandry, too tedious here to describe, many of which were of his own contrivance. He takes a visible pleasure in the study of agriculture, and in rural improvements, of which the valley of Glen Shira is a convincing proof. How creditable a pursuit this, compared with those which many of our inferior nobility delight themselves in ! And how happy is the county of Argyll in having such a man placed in the middle of it, whose inclination to do good is as ample as his power of doing it ! His venerable age, the sweetness and simplicity of his manners, with the cheerful alacrity showed by every one of the family to his easy commands are really delightful. He is indeed, in the fullest sense of the word, a father to his country. The numerous tenants on his extensive estates, both on the mainland and in the isles, are all gentlemen, even those of the smallest kind are easy in circumstances, happy in their families, and have an implicit confidence in the integrity of their illustrious chief, and every one of them, I daresay in cases of urgency would follow him or Lorne to the field, nor will it be every foe that will keep it, *when the Campbells are coming.*

I had heard it abroad that a man's disposition was best known by the characters of the people whom he had chosen to act under him; I was happy to find that here they were not all Mr. —— There is a Colonel Graham, whom I was only a few minutes in company with at the village, in whom the Duke placeth an unlimited confidence; and he hath the character of being every way worthy of it.   He is certainly a very superior man in every respect.

I was truly ashamed of the attention paid to me by Colonel Campbell.   He was indefatigable in his endeavours to make me understand the use and the meaning of every thing, both within and without the castle, made his sister again and again play upon the organ, because I admired it; led me through the whole castle to the very battlements; through every walk of the gardens; every corner of the large barns; and all the office houses; to the very dog-kennel; and made me give names to two young dogs, which I called Suwarrow and Lion.   It is a question if ever they were more minded; but this reminds me of an anecdote which I shall here relate.   ' How is that young dog of mine so much leaner than the others? said Colonel Campbell to the keeper. "I don't know," said he.   "You don't know !   But you ought to be better to mine."   " No," said he pertly, " I will be as good to Mr. Robert's as to yours."   " Aye," said the Colonel, " but you act like a puppy in being better to any man's dogs than your master's."   The lad looked this way and that way; patted the dog on the head, and had no answer.   When the other saw that,

he gave him half a crown for being so good to his brother's dog.'
Colonel Campbell also walked many miles through the woods and
fields with me, in order to give me the most advantageous views
of the different scenery surrounding that celebrated place, until
he was sometimes extremely warm, and he would not suffer me to
turn my eyes that way until he came to certain places in order
that the view might burst on me all at once, and which he
believed to be greatly assisting in the effect it produced.

One day when he wished that the environs of Loch Dow and
Glen Shira should open to me all at once, that I might not see it
by halves as we advanced, he placed his huge bulk on that side
of me, laid his arm on my shoulder, and repeated a piece of a
poem with great emphasis.   On one of these excursions we were
overtaken, and taken up into an open carriage by her ladyship
and some of her companions, which afforded us a much more easy
and agreeable conveyance.

I will not tell you all the remarks which I made upon this
celebrated lady, else people would refrain in future from introducing me to their wives or daughters in any case; thinking I
was just come to take observations.   There was one thing I
heard her assert, and in the presence of her husband too; that
she was a great admirer of you.   But you need not read this to
Mrs. Scott.

But of all the predicaments I ever got into, that of the theatre
excelled !   I suspect it was you that put it into their heads, else
they would never have set as many people to work a whole fore-

D

noon, lighting up, cleaning, and arranging the scenery of the theatre that I might judge of the fitness and propriety of each. Every new scene that was displayed, my judgment was asked in full council, of every particular part. Forgive me if I knew what to say! I had often no other answer ready than scratching the crown of my head. I cursed in my heart the hour that I first put my observations on the stage on paper; and like the Yorkshire man, wished all their canvas in *h*—— *bournin !*

The whole of this theatre, with all its appurtenances, is the contrivance, and executed under the direction of the Hon. Colonel Campbell. He is very proud of it, as indeed he very well may, for though small, it is a most finished little piece. No man would believe that he had such a taste for the fine arts as it is evident he hath, particularly in music and painting. I must again here draw my score, after subscribing myself, your humble servant,

J. H.

———

DEAR SIR,—In my last I began giving you an account of a ride which I had in company with Mr. ——, but fell through the subject, and never more minded* it. I will now, however, resume it, that you may see how unlucky I was in all my manœuvres among the nobility. I told you I was mounted on a

---

* Remembered.

fine mare ; I know not who she belonged to, but I never think it was the same that the Colonel ordered for me.   She was so full of spirits that every little rivulet, and every hillock that we came at, she must necessarily make a spring over it as if she had been passing over a six bar gate.   Yea, so intent was she on showing her prowess, that she bore me over dykes and ditches, than cross-ing which nothing could be more foreign to my inclinations or purpose.   I was almost driven to desperation by her behaviour, for on coming to the outside of a high faced wall on the east side of Glen Dow, and drawing near to look at a herd of roes that were feeding within, I had taken no notice of my beast, for in a moment she sprung forward, plunged over the dyke, and landed me on the inside, among the deer.   It was with much difficulty that I retained my seat, and being very angry, I whipped her against the dyke on the inside.   ' Now, jump that if you can.' I was very glad to find that Mr. ―― was in haste to get home. He could have no greater desire for it than I had.   Although I never said much he saw my condition well enough; and always added fuel to the fire by putting the spurs to his beast on pretence of trying a trot.   But then I would mine?   Not a step; but galloping, rearing, and running here-away-there-away.   I how-ever got back and got rid of her with whole bones, but well bathed in sweat.

I told you that they were rather inferior sheep that I saw.   I was, however, assured that the Duke had some most excellent parcels of Scottish wedders on the outer hills.   These I was to have seen the ensuing day, but I thought I had seen enough about Inveraray; at least before I saw as much about every place which I intended to visit, the year would be done. There was also a flock of sheep, composed of the largest Southern breeds, feeding on the castle bank. They were the strongest and best that ever I saw in Scotland, yet I was not displeased to hear that these were killed only for the use of the servants, and that the Scotch wedders were preferred for the Duke's table.

I could tell you a great deal more about this place, but I am sure you think I have descended too much to particulars already. I could tell you how struck I was on entering the library. How I could not perceive one book at all; how I always lost myself in the castle, and could never recognize the very rooms that I had lately left. And after all, there is nothing else left for me to write about. To attempt a general description after those of a Kaimes, a Pennant, and a thousand others, would be the highest presumption, and indeed I hate to write about that which everybody writes about. I shall only observe (and I am afraid that you will attribute it to a spirit of contradiction, or a pride in retaining my character of singularity), that I do not much admire the *natural scenery* of Inveraray. There is a sort of sameness in the extensive view of the opposite side of the lake, and even in the lake itself, being much of a width, and destitute of islands. The hill of Duniqueich, rising above the plain, hath something . of a romantic appearance, and is an exception to this general surmise; yet, strip the whole of its woods and lawns, and the

scene is just common enough.   But on the other hand, the arti-
ficial part is truly admirable, I had almost said inimitable.   The
elegant little town, the magnificent castle, the accurate taste, and
discernment exhibited in the formation of the lawns and groves,
many of which are striking copies of nature, and above all the
great extent of the policies, ever will be admired, and never will
be enough admired.

I was best pleased with the view of the castle from the lake,
when it appeared embosomed in woods, and was so well contrasted
with the village on one side, and a distant view of the majestic
mountains in a circular range beyond it.   But the greatest
beauty of all is this; and it is alike applicable to the policies, to
the castle, and to its inhabitants, that the nearer you approach,
the better the effect.   The closer the inspection, the more
exalted your admiration; and the better acquaintance, the greater
your esteem.   And though the Duke's great age hath certainly
considerably impaired the faculties of his mind, as well as his
body, yet during the short time that I was in his presence, I
could discover in the most trivial acts his unbounded generosity
and condescension.   I shall only mention one or two of those.

One. day at dinner Colonel Campbell said, ' My lord, why will
you not try the herrings?   It was for you that I ordered them.'
' Was it indeed, Jack ?' said he, ' then I certainly will try them.'
Which he did, and recommended them greatly.   After dinner
the ladies were diverting themselves by throwing crumbs of cake
at the gentlemen, and at one another, to make them start when

they were not observing.   His Grace was growing drowsy, and
one, wishing to rouse him up, called aloud in a weeping tone,
'Master, speak to Charlotte, she won't sit in peace.'   The good
old peer, to carry on the school jest, or rather the idea of the
farmer's table, turning to that side with an important nod, said,
'Be quiet, Charlotte, I tell you,' and smiling, laid himself back
on his easy chair again.   These are very trifling incidents, my
dear Sir, but by such little family anecdotes, genuine and unaffected, the natural disposition is easier to be recognized than
by a public action done in the face of the world.

But if I go backward and forward this way I shall never get
from Inveraray ; therefore suppose me all at once on the road
early in the morning on which I proceeded up Glen Aray,
viewed two considerable cataracts romantically shrouded in woods,
and at length arrived on the borders of Loch Awe, or Loch
Howe.   My plan was to take breakfast at Port Sonachan, and
proceed to Oban that night, having letters to some gentlemen of
that country, and having a pocket travelling map, I never asked
the road of anybody, at which indeed I have a particular
aversion, as I am almost certain of being obliged to answer
several impertinent questions as an equivalent for the favour
conferred.

The road that turns to the left toward Port Sonachan is
certainly in danger of being missed by a stranger, for although I
was continually on the look-out for a public road to that hand, I
never observed it in the least, till at last, seeing no ferry across

the lake, nor road from the other side, I began to suspect that I had erred, and condescended to ask of a man if this was the road to Port Sonachan. He told me that I was above a mile past the place where the roads parted. 'And where does this lead?' said I. 'To Tyndrum, or the braes of Glenorchy,' said he; and attacked me with other questions in return, which I was in no humour to answer, being somewhat nettled at missing my intended route, and more at missing my breakfast, but knowing that whatever road I took, all was new to me, I, without standing a moment to consider of returning, held on as if nothing had happened.

About eleven A.M. I came to Dalmally in Glenorchy, where I took a hearty breakfast, but the inn had a poor appearance compared with what I had left. Some of the windows were built up with turf, and, on pretence of scarcity of fuel, they refused to kindle a fire in my apartment, although I was very wet, and pleaded movingly for one. There was nothing in this tract that I had passed deserving of particular attention. The land on the south-east side of the lake is low-lying, interspersed with gentle rising hills, and strong grassy hollows, where good crops of oats and beans were growing. On the other side the hills are high and steep, and well stocked with sheep. One gentleman is introducing a stock of the Cheviot breed on a farm there this season. They had formerly been tried on a farm in the neighbourhood of the church, but the scheme was abandoned in its infancy.

I am, yours, etc.,

J. H.

DEAR SIR,—Leaving Dalmally, and shortly after, the high road to Tyndrum, I followed a country road which kept near the bank of the river, and led me up through the whole of that district called *the braes of Glenorchy*. At the bridge of Orchy, (or as it is spelled by some Urguhay), I rejoined the great military road leading to Fort William, and three miles farther on reached Inverournan, the mid-way stage between Tyndrum and the King's house beyond the Black Mount, where I took up my lodgings for the night.

The braes of Glenorchy have no very promising appearance, being much over-run with heath, and the north-west side rocky. But it is probable that I saw the worst part of them, their excellency as a sheep range having for a long time been established; for who, even in the south of Scotland, hath not heard of the farms of Soch and Auch!

The Orchy is a large river and there are some striking cascades in it. The glen spreads out to a fine valley on the lower parts, which are fertile, the soil on the river banks being deep, yet neither heavy nor cold. As you ascend the river the banks grow more and more narrow, till at last they terminate in heather and rocks. Beside one of the cascades which I sat down to contemplate, I fell into a long and profound sleep. The Earl of Breadalbane is the principal proprietor. I was now, at Inverournan, and got into a very Highland and rather a dreary scene. It is situated at the head of Loch Tullich, on the banks of which there yet remains a number of natural firs, a poor remembrance of the extensive woods with which its environs have once been over-run.

Amongst the fellow lodgers, I was very glad at meeting here with a Mr. M'Callum, who had taken an extensive farm on the estate of Strathconnon, which I viewed last year; who informed me, that all that extensive estate was let to sheep farmers, saving a small division on the lower end, which the General had reserved for the accommodation of such of the natives as could not dispose of themselves to better advantage.

Next morning I traversed the Black Mount in company with a sailor, who entertained me with many wonderful adventures; of his being pressed, and afterwards suffering a tedious captivity in France.   This is indeed a most dreary region, with not one cheering prospect whereto to turn the eye.   But on the right hand lies a prodigious extent of flat, barren muirs, interspersed with marshes and stagnant pools; and on the left, black rugged mountains tower to a great height, all interlined with huge wreaths of snow.   The scenery is nothing improved on approach-ing to the King's house.   There is not a green spot to be seen, and the hill behind it to the westward is still more terrific than any to the south of it, and is little inferior to any in the famous Glencoe behind it.   It is one huge cone of mishapen and ragged rocks, entirely peeled bare of all soil whatever, and all scarred with horrible furrows, torn out by the winter torrents.   It is indeed a singular enough spot to have been pitched upon for a military stage and inn, where they cannot so much as find forage for a cow, but have their scanty supply of milk from a few goats, which brouse on the wide waste.   There were, however, some very good black-faced wedder hoggs feeding in the middle of the Black Mount, but their colour and condition both, bespoke them to have been wintered on a richer and lower pasture, and only to have been lately turned out to that range.

After leaving the King's house I kept the high way leading to Balachulish for about two miles, and then struck off, following the old military road over the devil's stairs, which winds up the hill on one side and down on the other, and at length entered Lochaber by an old stone bridge over a water at the head of Loch Leven; and without meeting with anything remarkable, arrived at Fort William about seven o'clock p.m.

It is upwards of twenty miles from the King's house to Fort William, across the hills, and the road being extremely rough, my feet were very much bruised.   The tract is wild and mountainous, the hills on the Lochaber side are amazingly high and steep, and, from the middle upward, are totally covered with small white stones.   They form a part of that savage range called *the rough bounds*.   Before reaching the town I passed some excellent pasture hills which were thick covered with ewes and lambs.

On arriving at Fort William I went to the house of Mr. Thomas Gillespie, who left our south country about twenty years ago, and in partnership with another, took a farm from Glengarry.   His conditions were reasonable, and he being the first who introduced the improved breed of Scottish sheep into that district, his advantages were numerous, especially as his landlord, who had certainly been endowed with a liberality of mind and views extending far beyond the present moment, exacted no rent until it was raised from the farm. His companion soon gave up his share, but Mr. Gillespie, with a perseverance almost peculiar to himself, continued to surmount every difficulty, and at the expiration of every lease commonly added something to the extent of his possessions. He is now the greatest farmer in all that country, and possesseth a track of land extending from the banks of Loch Garey to the shores of the Western Ocean, upward of twenty miles.

Having lost a farm on which his principal residence stood he is now residing in Fort William, which any man would consider as very inconvenient; as so indeed it would be to any man save Gillespie, who is privileged with a person as indefatigable and unconquerable as his mind. He can sleep in the shepherds' cots for months together, and partake of their humble fare with as much satisfaction as the best lodgings and cheer in the world could bestow, and indeed he appears to be much happiest among his shepherds. I staid there with him two days, and saw everything about the fortress and village that were worth looking at; and as I cannot describe the garrison, by not knowing the terms used in fortification, there is nothing that falls to be particularly noticed here, if we except the large and very ancient castle of Inverlochy. It is a large square building, with four proportionally large turrets, one at each corner, but that looking toward the north-west is much the largest; but Mr. Stuart, the tenant at Inverlochy, with whom I dined one day and breakfasted another, had four most elegant daughters, whom I confess I admired much more than the four turrets of the castle. The name of this place is said only twice to occur in all the records of Scotland, and these at a very early period. It was there where the long respected treaty was signed between the Emperor Charlemagne and Achaius, King of Scotland. No traces of the town remain, though it is believed to have once been the capital of the Scots; nor was even the place where it stood known, until lately that on digging for stones a considerable pavement was raised behind some knolls, a little to the southward of the castle.

I was uncommonly intent on being at the top of Ben Nevis, which is agreed by all to be the highest mountain in the British Islands, but the mist never left its top for two hours during my stay. I had once set out and proceeded a good way toward it when the clouds again settled on its summit and obliged me to return.

Fort-William, or Maryburgh as it was formerly called, is situated on the side of Loch Yel, immediately at the confluence of the Nevis; and as the loch will admit ships of any burden, we might expect that from its favourable situation, it would be the mart of the whole Western Highlands; whereas it is destitute of trade and manufactures, nor was there a vessel in the harbour;

and there is thrice as much traffic and barter carried on at some of the fishing villages.

DEAR SIR,—Having breakfasted early we, viz., Mr. Gillespie, Mr. William Stuart of Inverlochy, and *Master James Hogg*, left Fort William.   Leaving the military road, we crossed the Lochy above the old castle.   It is a large, dark river, and there is a good salmon fishing in it, which is farmed by Mr. Stuart at a high rent, from the Duke of Gordon; but, like most of the northern rivers in the Western Highlands, hath failed unaccountably for two years past.   We kept by the side of the river and Loch Lochy until we came to the river Arkaig; then following its course, we reached Achnacarry, where we spent the middle of the day, viewing the new castle of Lochiel, the building of which was then going briskly on, conducted by Mr. John Gillespie, architect; a respectable young man, possessed of much professional knowledge, who kept us company during our stay.

The castle is on an extensive scale and promiseth to be a stately structure.   It is founded within a few yards of the site of the ancient one, the residence of the brave Lochiel who was wounded at the battle of Culloden, and escaped with Prince Charles to France.   This pile was reduced to ashes by the Duke of Cumberland's forces in seventeen hundred and forty-six, and the marks of the fire are still too visible, not only on the remaining walls of the house and offices, but also on a number of huge venerable trees, which the malevolent brutes had kindled. Some of these, although the heart was burnt out of them, still continued to flourish.

It is indeed a very remarkable spot to have chosen for erecting such a princely residence upon, being entirely obscured amongst woods and wild mountains, which deprive it of any prospect whatever. There is no public road near it, nor is it accessible by a carriage at present, yet I could not but in my heart greatly applaud Lochiel for the choice, not only as it was the seat of his noble ancestors, and adorned by a garden inferior to few in the Highlands, if again in repair, as well as by sundry elegant avenues, formed and shaded by trees of great age and beauty; but also on account of the utility of having his family residence in the midst of his extensive estate, in the very place where roads and bridges are most wanted, and where he can encourage by his example, elegance and improvements among the better part of his tenants, (many of whom are substantial, intelligent men of his own name,) give employment to the meaner sort, and assistance to the indigent. The whole scene is romantic beyond conception. On the banks of Loch Arkaig to beyond it there are large forests of wood, which in many places are perfect thickets. In these woods the Pretender skulked for some time, attended by a very few followers indeed, and was often in great danger of being surprised. He was in an island in Loch Arkaig when the corpse was found which was mistaken for the body of his dear Lochiel, and pained him beyond measure. It turned out to be only that of a friend of his. Lochiel remained safe and almost unmolested, amongst the wilds which separate Athol and Badenoch.

About one o'clock we took our leave of Mr. Stuart, Mr. Gillespie, the architect, and a Captain Cameron who had joined us, proceeded by the way of Glenkekuich, a most shocking road, where I thought Mr. Gillespie should have lost his horse. We were shown the very spot in this track where Prince Charles met a band of dragoons in search of him, and was forced to squat among the heath until they passed by, and was so near them that he heard their talk.

While traversing the scenes where the patient sufferings of the one party, and the cruelties of the other, were so affectingly displayed, I could not help being a bit of a Jacobite in my heart, and blessing myself that, in those days, I did not exist, or I should certainly have been hanged.

This country of Lochaber, which I now left behind me, excels all in those regions for lofty mountains and fertile valleys. It is upon the whole a very interesting and diversified scene, and were it not for my oath of brevity, I should certainly launch out into a particular description of it. The famous mountain of Ben Nevis, the king of the Grampians, rises 4380 feet above the level of the sea, and hugs in its uncouth bosom, huge masses of everlasting snow, and all that range, both to the east and west, is wild and savage beyond measure. The valleys are interspersed with numbers of cottages, as also a good many gentlemen's seats, and substantial houses belonging to the principal tenants, or rather tacksmen, as they are there denominated.   It is watered by the Nevis, the Lochy, the Spare, and the Arkaig ; and by numberless smaller streams.   In the more remote glens there are large and beautiful woods.   The estate of Letterfinlay, and some of Lochiel's glens are beautiful for sheep pasturage, but the bulk of the hills are rough and ugly.   There are a great many of the sheep not yet of a proper breed, and consequently not excellent, yet numbers of very strong wedders are annually driven to the south from some of these parts.

It is certainly a place where a great deal may be done, and where a great deal will be done.   The tillage is capable of being greatly extended, and if proper encouragement be given in the new leases, (for the most part of Lochaber is out of lease,) it will be extended, as well as improved.   As it is all on a Western exposure,   and   intersected   by   extensive   arms   of   the   sea, so remarkable for the humidity and freshness of its breezes, it suffers very little from storms of lying snow, for although the mountains are so very high, the bottoms of the glens seldom rise to any great height above the level of the sea ; so that in this important matter of snow storms the sheep farmer is safe.

The greater part of this district is certainly calculated only for the rearing of these useful animals, sheep, yet there are still many places not stocked with them, or but very partially so. But as there is now such a number of enlightened farmers in the country and its neighbourhood, experience, the most effectual teacher, will soon convince the natives of their real interest.

The Duke of Gordon, and Lochiel, are the principal proprietors. Glen Nevis, and Letterfinlay are also considerable estates.   IIis Grace's lands are rather overstocked with poor people.

It appears as if all these highland hills not many years ago, had been valued only in proportion to the game they produced, as the wildest and most uninhabitable countries never fail to belong to the greatest men.   The Duke of Gordon in particular, possesseth an immense range of these savage districts, extending in a confused chain from the Eastern to the Western Oceans. Take a journey through Lochaber, Laggan, Badenoch, Glenmore, and Strathaven, and when you come to a wild, desert glen, (and you will not miss *enow* of them,) you need not trouble yourself to enquire who is the proprietor.   You may take it for granted it is the 'Duke of Gordon,' and you would scarcely refrain from the Englishman's apostrophe to Invercauld, ' D—n that fellow, I believe he hath got the whole highlands.'

I promised to you at the first when I began to write to you on this subject that I would give my sentiments freely of men and things, whether they were right or wrong.   And I have to confess to you that my expectations with respect to the opening of the proposed canal, differ widely from those of almost every other person.   I have too high an opinion of the energy of the British Legislature to have any doubts of its accomplishment, but I will venture to predict that although you should live an

F

hundred years after its completion, you will never see it a well-frequented canal; nay, that you shall never see the tonnage pay the interest of the sum thereon expended. You will be apt to tear this letter or fling it away in a rage, but I charge you do not, but keep it, and when you die tell Walter to keep it until the result shall prove the absurdity of my ideas, and then do anything with it you please. I will in my next acquaint you with my simple reasons for this belief, as well as my hopes of its utility, which nevertheless in one sense are very sanguine.

In the meantime, believe me, Sir, your faithful,   J. H.

———

My Dear Sir,—I know that you will reject my arguments on this subject as futile and inadmissible, but I do not care. Enough hath been said and written on the other side, therefore I shall state my reason and let the event do justice to the merits of each calculator.

And in the first place I think that the greatest number of vessels may be supposed to pass by it from East to West, because those bound from America to any of the ports on the continent of Europe, or Eastern coast of Britain, could, while in the open Atlantic, steer with as much ease and safety by Orkney, as through amongst the Hebrides into Lochiel. Now, to counter-act this I must inform you of a circumstance which you probably have never thought of, but to the truth of which every sailor

coastwise, and every attentive shepherd in Scotland can bear
witness, that in a term of three years the wind always blows at
least two-thirds of the time from that quarter of the compass
lying betwixt South and West.   If these two points are allowed,
as in part they must, how is it possible to navigate these narrow
lochs with a continual head wind, where no tides are, to carry
them on piecemeal, as in the sounds of the ocean?   But granting, what is not possible, that the winds as well as the navigation
should be equal from each side of the island, yet, in Loch Ness
especially, the hills spreading at each end, and the whole length
of the lake being confined between two steep ridges of mountains,
the wind must necessarily blow either straight up or straight
down the lake, consequently the sailor must enter the narrow
gut with the disagreeable assurance of having all the winds from
one half of the globe right ahead of him.   I acknowledge myself
to be quite ignorant of the principles of navigation, but the idea
of conducting a heavy ship in this case betwixt two rocky shores
never above a mile, and often not above half a mile separated,
appears to me a desperate undertaking.

    The argument that there are a number of safe anchorings, is
of small avail either for safety or despatch.   They are indeed a
safeguard against a continued storm, but none against sudden
squalls, which amongst the mountains and gaps are as terrible as
they are unceasing ; and it would be no very agreeable circumstance for a heavy ship to be overtaken by one of these, augmented with the united gusts from several glens while endea-

vouring to tack, so hard upon a lea shore as they must of necessity be, if indeed they get any stretch at all.

I wish from my heart, sir, that these impediments may be
only imaginary, and I shall try to console myself with the assurance that they were all weighed by more experienced heads
ere ever the experiment was seriously thought of.

In one case I am sure it will in time prove a national benefit,
namely by drawing a numerous population into that important
isthmus, formed by nature to be the seat of trade betwixt the
countries to the south and north of it.   At different places
along it, and at different seasons, there should be large trysts
established for cattle and sheep, corresponding with those in the
south, that the farmers in the highlands and islands to the north
of that may not be so entirely in the power of interested drovers,
who, though an useful set of men, get a great deal of the cattle
and sheep in those distant countries on their own terms.   They
are so far removed from any principal market that the people
for the most part, rather than set out toward the banks of the
Forth with their own small quantity, prefer such offers as come
to their own doors, though often very inferior, there being also a
risk of late and uncertain payment, whereas were they sure of
even a moderate price for driving them to the banks of Glen-
more-na-h-alabin, it would be a great encouragement.   Besides,
they would from the same place need frequent supplies of many
of the necessaries, and all the luxuries of life, as from thence
they could have easy conveyances either by land or water.

But you will readily ask, from whence shall this population and increased traffic proceed, if, as you say, it is not to be influenced by an extensive business carried on by the canal?   My dear sir, you are not aware what prodigious numbers of poor people drag on a wretched existence in those distant glens and islands, who are scarcely privileged, as we would think, with one of the comforts or conveniences of life.   As for instance, what do you think of upwards of ten thousand people subsisting on the dreary and distant Isle of Lewis, which with the exception of a very inconsiderable part, is one extensive morass; while the whole rent of the island, although lately advanced, does not reach to a thousand pounds.   This is but one instance out of many, and it may well be supposed, nay, I am *certain*, that there are many thousands in these countries whose condition cannot be *worsed* unless they are starved to death.   Now, only conceive what numbers of these, from first to last, will be employed here before the great canal and the roads be finished, where they will mix with more enlightened people, form acquaintances, contract marriages, and thus enlarge their connections in the place.   New lights and advantages, both real and imaginary, will daily present themselves to their imaginations, as acquirable in that place where conditions have been ameliorated by their application to labour, so that we may presume that a small encouragement held out to such as choose to settle in the great glen, will readily be accepted of by numbers.

Perhaps a prejudiced fellow like me, unconscious of the utility of such a naval communication, may think that one third of the money laid out upon the great canal, would have been better employed in purchasing land to be let out in feus to those tribes and families annually, vomited out by their own native, inhospitable shores, and forced to seek for a more certain means of subsistence in the Western world, in search of which, many a brave Scot has sunk broken-hearted and forlorn, to his long home, and has found the wished-for resting place only in the New World, beyond death and the grave, while the last idea that floated on his distempered mind, and the last words that wavered on his tongue, were those of regard for his native land.

And after all, if something is not done to provide asylums for these brave men and their families, and to establish woollen manufactures, they may live to see their *roads grow green, and a blue scum settle on their canal;* and to hear themselves addressed in the language of Scripture, Matthew, xxiii., and 23. 'Woe be to you, ye blind guides, who strain at a gnat, and swallow a camel! These things ought ye to have done, and not to have left the other undone."

Rest assured of this, my dear sir; that men, sheep, and fish, are the great staple commodities of Scotland; and that, though a number of other improvements *may* contribute to its emolument, yet whatever tends more particularly to encourage or improve any of these *will* do it.

I shall probably have occasion to treat more of this in another place, and shall again proceed on my journey.

On reaching Glengarry the first place we came to was Green-
field, possessed by Mr. M'Donald.   The house was really a
curiosity.   It was built of earth, and the walls were all covered
with a fine verdure, but on calling we were conducted into a
cleanly and neat-looking room, having a chimney, and the walls
being plastered.   The ladies, Mrs. M'Donald and her sister,
were handsome and genteelly dressed, although unapprised of our
arrival, unless by the second sight. They were very easy and agreeable in their manners, and very unlike the *outside* of their habitation. The family were Roman Catholics, and kept a young priest
among them, but he had lately been obliged to abscond for some
misdemeanour in marrying a couple secretly. He was much
lamented by the whole family, but by none so much as Miss
Flora.

We saw Mr. M'Donald's ewes gathered.   He hath an excellent
stock of sheep.   We got a late dinner, drank plenty of punch,
etc., and at night crossed the Garry to Inchlaggan, a farm of
Mr. Gillespie's and took up our lodging with his shepherd.

I remain, your most affectionate servt.,

J. H.

———

DEAR SIR,—I took leave of you in my last at Inchlaggan in
Glen Garry, where Gillespie and I slept together in a small
stooped bed, having neither sides nor cover. We spent the whole

of next day among his sheep, came back to the same lodgings at night, and the third day I took my leave of him, very well pleased with what I had seen.   It is believed by most people that I am too partial to the Highlands, and that they will not produce such stocks as I affirm that they will.   Let them only take an impartial view of Glengarry and accuse me if they can.   The superiority of its grazings to those of a great many other Highland countries, is in no wise discernable to the beholder, yet the stocks of sheep upon it are equal in quality to those of any country in the south of Scotland.   Gillespie hath one farm completely stocked with the finest Cheviot breed, which thrive remarkably well.   These he bought on the Border, at the exhorbitant prices of sixteen shillings for each lamb, and twenty-four for each of the hoggs, or year-olds.   The lambs came all safe home, but three of the hoggs fell by the way.   They went home on the seventeenth day from their leaving Rule Water, a distance upwards of two hundred miles by the drove road.   He intends breeding wedders from them for his farms of Glenqueich, but to sell the ewe lambs until he sees how the wedders thrive.   All the stocks of sheep on Glengarry are good, the farms belong all to Mr. Gillespie, or have been possessed by him, consequently the sheep are all of his breed.   The ground lets very high. Alexander Macdonald, Esquire, of Glengarry, is the proprietor. A great part of the land is very coarse, but the heather, grass, and all sorts of herbage grow luxuriantly, and spring up to a great length.   There is a considerable part of flat ground, and some woods on the lower parts, and the hills are lower and of easier ascent than those of Lochaber.

Leaving Inchlaggan and Mr. Gillespie, I travelled through an exceedingly rough country. The day was wet and misty, and there was no track of a road, or if there was I did not happen on it. I crossed Glen-Loyn hard by the mouth of the loch; went through a farm belonging to Ratachan, which was very coarse land, being overrun with moss, but on which there was a very excellent stock of wedders feeding. After a most fatiguing march, I came in upon Loch-Cluny, and crossing the water at its head, I joined the old military road at the very green spot where Dr. Johnson rested, and first conceived the design of transmitting his tour to posterity.

I came to the house of Cluny, which is a solitary steading in that wild glen. It is a change-house, but I did not know, nor even thought of it, although I had much need of some refreshment. There were sundry workmen employed in mounting a house, at whom I only enquired the road; but I had not proceeded many miles until I grew faintish with hunger, having got nothing that day, saving a little pottage at the shepherd's house, early in the morning.

The road down Glen Shiel is entirely out of repair and remarkably rough and stony, and I was quite exhausted before I reached any other house, which was not until about the setting of the sun. I at length came to a place where there had been a great number of houses, which were now mostly in ruins, the

G

estate being all converted into sheep-walks. I went into the best
that remained, and immediately desired them to give me some
meat. I was accosted by an old man who declared that they had
nothing that they could give me. I told him that it was with
much difficulty I had got that length, and that I was not able to
proceed further unless I got something to eat, and desired him to
order me something, for which I was willing to pay whatever he
should demand. He persisted in his denial of having anything
that he could give me, telling me that I was not two miles from
the change-house. I was obliged to go away, although I suspected that I would not *make* the inn, but before I had gone far
a young man came out and called me back. He was in a poor
state of health, and had risen out of his bed on hearing the
dialogue between the old man and me. He conducted me into
a kind of room, and presented me with plenty of bread, whey,
butter, and cheese. In the state that I was in, I durst only take
a very little, for which he refused to take anything, declaring
that I was very welcome, and that he wished the fare had been
better, for my sake. I was greatly refreshed, and proceeded on
my way. Before it was quite dark I reached the inn of Inver-
shiel, or Shiel-house, held by a Mr. Johnston from Annandale.
It is a large, slated house, but quite out of repair, and the
accommodations are intolerably bad. The lower apartments are
in utter confusion, and the family resides in the dining-
room above. Consequently, they have only one room into
which they thrust promiscuously every one that comes. The

plaister of this being all discoloured, and full of chinks, the eye is continually tracing the outlines of monstrous animals and hobgoblins upon it. I got the best bed, but it was extremely hard, and the clothes had not the smell of roses. It was also inhabited by a number of little insects common enough in such places, and no sooner had I made a lodgement in their hereditary domains than I was attacked by a thousand strong. But what disturbed me much worse than all, I was awaked during the night by a whole band of Highlanders, both male and female, who entered my room, and fell to drinking whisky with great freedom. They had much the appearance of a parcel of vaga-bonds, which they certainly were, but as the whole discourse was in Gaelic I knew nothing of what it was concerning, but it arose by degrees as the whisky operated, to an insufferable noise. I had by good fortune used more precaution that night than usual, having put my watch and all my money into my waistcoat and hid it beneath my head. I also took my thorn-staff into the bed with me, thereby manifesting a suspicion that I had never shewed before. I bore all this uproar with patience for nearly two hours in the middle of the night, until, either by accident or design, the candle was extinguished, when every one getting up, a great stir commenced, and I heard one distinctly ransacking my coat which was hanging upon a chair at a little distance from the bed. I cared not much for that, thinking that he could get nothing there, but not knowing where this might end I sprung to my feet in the bed, laid hold of my thorn-staff, and bellowed aloud for light. It was a good while ere this could be procured, and when it came the company were all gone but three men, who were making ready to lie down in another bed in the same room. I reprimanded the landlord with great bitterness for suffering such a disturbance in the room where I slept, and received for answer that all would be quiet now. They were all gone before I got up next morning, and it was not until next night that I perceived I had lost a packet of six letters which I carried, to as many gentlemen in Sutherland, and which prevented me effectually from making the tour of that large and little-frequented county. These being rolled up in a piece of paper by themselves and lodged in my breast pocket, some one of the gang had certainly carried off in expectation that it was something of more value. Next day I went to the house of Ratagan or Ratachan, possessed by Donald Macleod, Esquire, to whom I had a letter of introduction. He received me with that open, unaffected, cordiality which is a leading trait in his character, and without that state and ceremony which is certainly often carried too far by the Highland people, and which I hate above all things. His conversation was much confined to that which suited me best, namely, the sheep-farming. He hath extensive concerns in this way, being possessed of two large farms here in Glen Shiel, exclusive of that of Armidel in Glen Elg, or as they pronounce it, Glen Ellig, which he had lately taken at the yearly rent of £600. He had the best wedder hoggs without exception that I saw in my whole journey. He bought them as lambs from Killetur in Glenfalloch.   He remembered Dr. Johnson and Mr. Boswell, and told me sundry anecdotes relating to them.   His mother is still alive, a woman of a great age yet quite healthy.   She dined and supped with us, but did not converse any, which was probably owing to her inaccuracy in the English language.   She is the same of whom Dr. Johnson makes honourable mention in his tour.   We had plenty of music and some dancing, his eldest daughter being a most charming performer on the pianoforte, and Mr. Gordon, the family teacher, equally expert at playing on the violin.

I would willingly have staid some days in this agreeable family, but was afraid that Macleod's attention to me would retard the shearing of his flocks, for which he had everything in readiness ; so hearing that the Rev. John Macrae was bound for Ardhill in Lochalsh, I took my leave in order to accompany him.   Ratachan accompanied me to the manse, and left me in charge with the parson.   Here the company at dinner consisted of twelve, which, saving the old minister and I, were all ladies ; mostly young ones, and handsome.   As soon as dinner was over, we entered into a boat, viz., Miss Flora Macrae of Ardintoul, and her aunt, the parson, and me.   Miss Flora was tall, young and handsome, and being dressed in a dark riding habit, with a black helmet and red feather, made a most noble figure.   I was very happy on hearing that she was to be a passenger.   We had six rowers in the boat, and *we* sat in a row astern, the two ladies being *middlemost.*   There being a sharp breeze straight in our face, as soon as we were seated, Mr. Macrae spread his great coat on the old lady and himself. This was exactly as I wished it, and I immediately wrapped Miss Flora in my shepherd's plaid, and though I was always averse to sailing, I could willingly have proceeded in this position at least for a week. We were at length obliged to put ashore about the middle of Loch Duich, at the place to which the boat belonged, but as I have drawn out this letter to an enormous length, I will bid you adieu for a few days.—Yours, etc.,

J. H.

DEAR SIR,—No sooner had the boat touched the shore than we were met by the owner, who was in uncommonly high spirits, that being his wedding-day. He insisted on our staying to drink tea with him, and to induce us to comply told us that if we staid we should have the boat and crew all the way, but if we refused to countenance him we should walk all the rest of the way on foot. There was no resisting this proposal so we went ashore, drank tea with the young couple and their friends, and so strongly did they press us to drink whisky, that had I been in company with any other than the minister and Miss Flora, they had certainly persuaded me to fill myself drunk. We then marched into the barn, where the music was playing, and joined with avidity in their Highland reels until reminded by Mr.

Macrae of approaching night, when we all again resumed our former berths in the boat and proceeded with as much cheerfulness as can be conceived. Mr. Macrae hath the character of being a very able divine, for which I cannot avouch, but he certainly is a most jocose and entertaining companion.

The family of Ardintoul being all Roman Catholics, thinking to lead me into a scrape when in the boat—

'Have you any priests in your country, Mr. Hogg?' said he.

'We have some very superior parish ministers in my country, sir,' said I.

'It is Popish priests that I mean,' said he, 'I hope you are not plagued with any of that wicked set.'

'There are none of that persuasion in my neighbourhood,' said I, 'saving the Earl of Traquair and his family, who keep a priest among them.'

'Ah! You are well quit of them,' said he, 'we are terribly plagued with them hereabouts! They are a bad set of people! Do you not think, Mr. Hogg, that they are very bad people?'

I began to suspect him. 'I don't know, sir,' said I, 'there are certainly worthy persons of every persuasion. I approve greatly of a person keeping to the religion in which he is brought up, and I would never esteem a man the less because he thought differently from me.'

The old lady then began to attack him, asking if ever he had found them to be ill neighbours.

'Oh! It won't do, it won't do!' said he, 'I thought of leading Mr. Hogg into a little abuse of you, as I once did a tide-waiter at your brother's house, who ignorant that his kind entertainer and the family were all of that persuasion, fell on and abused the Papists without either mercy or discretion, putting Ardintoul's great patience severely to the test. He was suffered, however, to depart in his error.'

We at length set the ladies ashore and took our leave of them. I gave Miss Flora two letters to her father, and promised to dine with them next day. Mr. Macrae, after taking leave of them, cried out shrewdly, 'Now farewell, Miss Flora! Without pretending to the spirit of prophecy I could tell you who you will dream of to-night.'

Considering of what inflammable materials my frame is composed, it was probably very fortunate that I was disappointed of ever seeing Miss Macrae again, as I might have felt the inconvenience of falling in love with an object in that remote country. I received word next day at Ardhill that she was taken very ill of the influenza, then raging in Kintail with great violence, and that Ardintoul, her father, was confined to bed, so that I was persuaded by the company to relinquish my intended visit as inconvenient.

About eight o'clock, p.m., we landed at Ardhill, the house of the Rev. Alexander Downie, minister of Lochalsh, to whom I had likewise a letter of introduction, from his cousin, Colin Mackenzie, Esquire, W.S. This district of Glen Shiel which I now had left, is like the greatest part of the countries on that coast, very mountainous.   Although the whole parish is thus denominated, Glen Shiel properly is that straight glen which terminates at the outer end of Loch Duich, and, stretching to the south-east, includes a great part of Glen Morison, and on the east is bounded by the heights of Affarick, one of the branches of the Glass.   The mountains are very high and steep, especially those of them most contiguous to the sea.   They are very rocky and often bare of soil, but the rocks are everywhere interlined with green stripes covered with sweet and nutritious grasses, which being continually moistened with fresh showers from the Atlantic, are preserved in verdure a great part of the year.   The snow never continues long on these mountains except on the heights, the frosts are seldom intense, but the winds and rains are frequent and terrible.   You will be apt to suppose that all that western coast will be alike exposed to these, but there is, according to the inhabitants, who must know best, a very great difference.   Wherever the mountains towards the shore rise to a great height there the rains are most frequent and descend in most copious abundance; and it is observed that places in the same latitude with these mountains on the eastern coast are very rarely visited with any rain from the west.   It is a fact that these mountains attract the clouds as well as intercept and break them, as I shall show in a future letter.   But there is no part of the Highlands to which the climate is better adapted than Glen Shiel, the hills being so steep and bare of soil, and so dry

H

naturally, that without a constant rain they would soon wither
and decay.

The mountains of Glen Shiel have been under sheep for some
years, of which I shall have occasion to treat farther at another
time.   The banks of Loch Duich are as yet mostly stocked with
cattle, and there is part arable land, which although not produc-
tive of weighty crops, produces them without much uncertainty.
Two gentlemen had sowed potatoe oats this season which looked
very well, and promise to answer the climate if they are cut in
time, before they are shaken by the winds.   The tract of land
stretching alongst the southern shore of Loch Duich, although
in the parish of Glen Shiel, is called Letterfern.   The banks of
this lake, which is an inlet of the sea from the Sound of Skye,
presents to the traveller many scenes of natural beauty.

· We sailed close under the walls of the ancient castle of Ellen-
donan, or the Sea-fort, the original possession of the family of the
Mackenzies, Earls of Seaforth, and from which they draw their
title.   The history of their first settling in that country after the
battle of Largs, of the manner of their working themselves into
the possession of Kintail, Loch Alsh, and Glen Shiel, and afterwards of Lewis, was all related to me by Mr. Macrae with great
precision.   It is curious and entertaining, but full of intrigue
and deceit, and much too tedious for me to write, as it would of
itself furnish matter for a volume.   The battle of Glen Shiel did
not happen until some years after the battles of Sherriffmuir and
Preston, and was fought near the boundaries of Seaforth's

country, in a strait pass between the mountains of Glen Shiel. The combatants were our King's troops and a body of about five or six hundred Highlanders and Spaniards, headed by the brave but misguided Earl of Seaforth.

The Spaniards, sensible of their destitute situation engaged reluctantly ; but seeing the intrepidity of the brave Macraes and Mackenzies, they maintained the combat stoutly for some time. The Highlanders say that the commander of the King's troops was killed, and that they were upon the very point of giving way when the Spaniards threw down their arms and surrendered, and that then the clansmen were obliged to betake themselves to flight, carrying with them from the field their lord, dangerously wounded.   He was then obliged to go into exile, and his lands were forfeited to the Crown, but the bold and tenacious inhabitants absolutely refused paying rents to any man excepting their absent chief, and all the endeavours of Government to collect them were baffled with disgrace.   Their agents were repelled and some of them slain, while the rents were regularly transmitted to the earl, and it showed the great lenity of our Government that they were not made examples of, and that the annals of that age were not stained with the massacre of Glenshiel, in addition to that of Glencoe.

I remain, Sir, yours for ever,

J. H.

DEAR SIR,—As I arrived at Ardhill on the Friday preceding the celebration of the sacrament of the Supper in that place, I was introduced to a whole houseful of ministers and elders. As Mr. Downie, however, kept an excellent board, and plenty of the best foreign spirits, we had most excellent fare, and during that night and the next day, which you know was the preparation day, we put ourselves into as good a state of preparation for the evening solemnity as good cheer would make us. To introduce you a little into our company, I will give you a sketch of our ministers.

Mr. Downie, our landlord, is a complete gentleman, nowise singular for his condescension. Besides the good stipend and glebe of Loch Alsh, he hath a chaplaincy in a regiment, and extensive concerns in farming, both on the mainland and in the isles, and is a great improver in the breeds both of cattle and sheep. Mr. Macrae of Glenshiel, as I before hinted, though advanced in years, is a most shrewd and good humoured gentle- man, whose wit never tends to mortify anybody, but only to raise the laugh against them. Mr. M'Queen of Applecross is a quiet, unassuming man. He is from the Isle of Skye, and is son to the minister there, who was so highly approved of by Dr. Johnson. Mr. Colin M'Iver of Glen Elig, was there on the Saturday, but was obliged to set off for Lewis to see a brother who was on his death-bed. He is a man whose presence commands respect. But the most extraordinary personage of the whole was a Mr. Roderick Macrae, preacher of the Gospel at Ferriden. He is certainly a

man of considerable abilities, but his manner is the most
singular, and his address the most awkward that were ever com-
bined in the same being.   He keeps his head in a continual up-
and-down motion, somewhat resembling a drake approaching his
mate, or a horse which has been struck violently on the head, and
who is afraid that you are going to repeat the blow; and at each
of these capers, he gives a strait wink with his eyes; and who-
ever is speaking, he continues at every breath to repeat a kind of
wince, signifying that he is taking notice, or that he wisheth you
to proceed.   Against this man all their shafts were levelled, often
armed with the most keen and ready wit.

Parish ministers in a country place, being so used to harangue
others, and to see whole multitudes turn up the white of the eye
to their discourse, are themselves so little used to listen to
others, that though they are often the best informed men of the
place and excellent single companions, very seldom is it that they
can make themselves agreeable in a larger company, as they only
wish to be listened unto, and never condescend to take any heed
to that which is said by others.   It was by such a behaviour
that this young man drew on himself the ridicule of the others
in one united torrent, for, as he engrossed at least one half of the
whole conversation, and as the rest were all his seniors, all of
them were chagrined at being superseded in their favourite
amusement of divulging their sentiments.

Mr. Downie, who is certainly a very clever man, as well as a
great scholar, took every opportunity to mortify and crush him.

Old Macrae set the whole table in a roar of laughter at him a hundred times ; and, indeed, I think I never laughed so much at a time in my life.   He had lately published a pamphlet, entitled 'A Dissertation on Miracles,' some copies of which were in the room, and proved matter for considerable rebuffs.   The piece itself was sound, simple reasoning and common sense, but every possible method was taken to wrest the sentiments, that the ideas might be turned into ridicule.   In particular, they objected, and not without considerable show of reason, that the whole of it went directly to counteract the intent of its publication, which being to confute the arguments of Mr. Hume, it would readily induce the country people, many of whom had never heard of Mr. Hume nor his book, to search for and consult it, when there was little doubt of their finding his arguments stronger and more impressive than those set down in the pamphlet.

Mr. Downie made me acquainted with the book and its author in the following brief manner.   Taking it off a back table, 'Here,' said he, 'Mr. Hogg, is a dissertation on *Miracles*, composed, written, and published by our friend Mr. Rory there, a certain evidence that miracles have not ceased.'   Mr. Roderick, however, stood his ground powerfully against them all, for he still kept his good temper—the best mark of an antagonist—persevered in his untoward motions, and in maintaining the excellence of his arguments.

Among such a number of literary men I could not miss getting a good deal of intelligence respecting the state of the countries in their different parishes, of which I made so little use that I dare not state one article as received from any of them; for, judging it ill manners to make out a journal of it in their company, I committed it wholly to my memory, where, setting it so effectually afloat on rum-punch, when I went to collect it I could only fish out some insignificant particles. There were no ladies in the room but Mrs. Downie, a beautiful little woman, exceedingly attentive to the accommodation of her guests, especially such as were bashful and backward. She was one of the Miss M'Kinnons of Corrialachan, in Skye.

On Saturday there was an extraordinary multitude assembled to hear sermon. I thought I never saw as many on the same occasion by one half, which convinced me that the lower classes of Kintail are devout. The men are generally tall and well made, and have good features. The women of the lower class are very middling.

The two Messrs. Macrae preached; the one in Gaelic at the tent, and the other in the church in English. By far the greatest congregation attended at the tent. There was, however, a considerable number of the more genteel people in the church. I was persuaded, much against my inclination, by the importunities of the minister, to officiate as precentor in the church that day, otherwise he must have acted in that capacity himself.

On returning to dinner our company was considerably augmented, so much that the circle went in contact with the walls of the dining-room. This made me alter my resolution of staying on the Sacrament, for fear of proving an incumbrance, which I would always avoid.   After dinner Mr. M'Kinnon, a young gentleman from Skye, and I, set off for the house of Auchtertyre, inhabited by Donald Macdonald, Esquire, of Barrisdale.   I saw and spoke with him and Mrs. Macdonald at church, and expected that they would invite me which, however, they did not.   The Highland gentlemen expect strangers to call without being invited.   I did not know this, but went to see the man merely because I liked him, for in conformity to a maxim of old Advocate Mackintosh's, ' *I never like a man if I don't like his face.*'

We met a most kind welcome from Barrisdale, whom we found in the midst of a great room-full of ladies, with only one or two young gentlemen, of whom he complained that they would not, drink any.   I have met again with the families of Ratachan and Glenshiel.   The drinking was renewed on our entering, which before had been going to fall into disuse, and we soon became remarkably merry, screwed up the fiddles, and raised a considerable dance.   It was here that I first ventured to sing my song of Donald Macdonald, which hath since become so popular, and although afraid to venture it I could not forbear, it was so appropriate, Barrisdale being one of the goodliest and boldest looking men anywhere to be met with.   It was so highly applauded here that I sung it very often during the rest of my journey.

By this excursion we missed the prayers and exhortations at

the manse, whither we returned to supper.   The supper did not, however, close the exercise of the evening, but as it is certainly time for me to close this letter, I shall write farewell.

I am, yours for ever,

J. H.

————

DEAR SIR,—Leaving Ardhill early in the morning, and climbing the mountains towards the country of Loch Carron, I took a last look of Kintail, not without regret, for I really admired the inhabitants as well as the country,   It is subdivided into several small districts, such as Glen Shiel, Glen Croe, Glen Elchaig, Letterfeirn and Loch Alsh, but the whole country is included in the general name of Kintail, or Lord Seaforth's country.   What a great pity it is that his circumstances have made it necessary for him to mutilate so fine and so compact an estate by selling Loch Alsh, the richest, and most beautiful part of it.

The whole is an excellent pasture country, and excels all that I visited on the whole Western coast of Scotland and the Isles, for the richness of its pasture, if we except some parts of Skye. The black cattle are a very handsome breed, but unless in Glen-Shiel the sheep farming is by no means become general as yet. Barrisdale and Ardintoul have both commenced it, bringing hoggs from the south.   I am very apprehensive that on being first stocked with sheep, the braxy will prove very destructive, for

I

exclusive of the *toth*, caused by such members of cattle feeding and lying upon it, the grasses are naturally flatulent, and the herbage indigestible, and as they have not all sea-marsh to lay them upon, the only preventatives that are in their power must be the effect produced by burning the ground well, and in the proper management of their flocks.

In the first place, as to burning their ground, they must be careful to lay waste by fire all or the greatest part of their heather that is upon clay or gravelly soils; such parts being without fail, of all others the most instrumental in raising the braxy. Whether this proceeds from the nature of the heather itself, or from the long, foul, grass that is always fostered about the roots of the bushes, I cannot so certainly determine. Perhaps it ariseth from both causes united; but in either respect the fire is an effectual remedy, and as the ground becomes annually more thickly covered with sweet blades, and sprays of grass which owing to the ashes with which it is sprinkled and impregnated, are all rather of a purgative nature, thus by the operation of burning alone, the very spots that were before the bane of the flocks are rendered the most conducive in preserving their health. Even when the young heather again begins to sprout, it is not for many years of a hurtful nature, but is a soft, and most palatable food. And as it is only in the first year of the sheep's age that they are subject in any great degree to this destructive malady, methods may be pursued in the arrangement of the flocks which may be greatly instrumental in allaying its virulence.

But as I rather wish to study brevity in these letters I shall reserve my suggestions on that head until a more suitable opportunity.

Loch Duich is an excellent fishing station, but there are neither villages, roads, bridges, nor post office, in the whole country. The gentlemen employ a runner to Loch Carron, where a foot-post arrives once a week from Inverness by the way of Strathconon, where he must often be detained by storms and flooded waters. The old military road, which runs through a corner of the upper parts of the country, leading to Fort-Augustus is, as I before observed, almost impassible, not having been repaired for ages; and all the others are entirely in a state of nature, being merely small tracks worn on the surface by the frequent pressure of the traveller's foot. In particular it was alleged to me that a road leading from the head of Loch Luang through the braes of Balloch into Strathglass would be of the greatest utility to both countries by opening the straightest and quickest communication betwixt the two seas.

Kintail is not much appropriated for the purposes of agriculture. It is indeed interspersed by vallies of small extent which are not of themselves unfertile, but the boisterousness of the weather, renders their produce very precarious.

The mountains in Glenshiel and Seaforth's forest viewed from the hills of Loch Alsh, although lofty and rugged have a verdant appearance. The mountains of Skye contiguous to the Kyles, appear much more dark. I came in upon Loch Carron at the

narrowest place, nigh where it opens to the sea, when there was
a boat just coming to land, freighted from a house several miles
up on the other side of the loch, by some people bound to the
place from whence I came.   I waited their arrival, thinking it a
good chance, but in this I was mistaken.   No arguments would
persuade them to take me along with them.   They alleged that
it was depriving the ferryman of his right.   But effectually to
remove this impediment, I offered them triple freight, but they
dared not to trust themselves with such a sum, for they actually
rowed off, and left me standing on the rocks, where I was obliged
to bellow and wave my hat for no small space of time.   The
ferryman charged sixpence and *a dram of whisky*.   I then kept
the North-west side of the loch, which stretcheth about ten miles
into the country, following a kind of formed road ; but on which
a wheeled carriage seemed never to have gone, nor had the
makers ever intended that it should.

    The hills on each side of the lake are of a moderate height, but
rise much higher as you advance into the country.   The arable
land was confined to very narrow limits, consisting of great numbers of small detached spots.   I was exceedingly gratified at here
meeting with a long, straggling village, consisting wholly of neat,
modern, commodious houses.   Having never heard of it, I made
enquiry concerning its erection, and was informed that it had
lately arisen under the auspices of Mackenzie of Applecross, who
had let it off in feus to the fishermen, and such as chose to settle
there.   This is a most laudable example set by this gentleman,

an example of which every reflecting mind must approve, and which can never be too much encouraged, either by individuals or by public bodies of men. It is only by concentrating these hardy and determined people into such bodies, that they shall ever be enabled to acquire the proper benefit of the inestimable fishings on their coasts, or that ever the germs of manufactures shall be successfully planted on these distant shores.

This spot pitched on by Applecross for so beneficial a purpose is not so commodious in every respect as it might be wished that it were ; but perhaps Applecross had no better. In this spot it is impossible to unite utility with compactness and elegance, for there being no valley the houses are drawn out in an irregular line along the side of the loch, and however well situated for taking advantage of trade and fishing, it is a very untoward field for improvements in agriculture.

Passing on, I went past the church, and through a carse, reaching New Kelso to my breakfast, a distance of nearly twenty miles from Ardhill.   This is a spacious house, with a well-stocked garden for such a soil.   It stands in the middle of a large, coarse plain, a great part of which is uncultivated, and which could only be cultivated with much labour.   The history of the erection of this place by Mr. Jeffery, and for what purpose, is too well known to need recapitulation here.

Proceeding up the glen, I lost sight of Loch Carron, crossed a rapid river which issued from amongst the hills to the north, saw numbers of Highland cottages in clusters, sheep, mostly of the

old Highland breed, and some goats, and at last came to a change-
house, of which I do not know the name, at the north-east corner
of a lake in the middle of the Strath. I recognised it as such by
a half-mutchkin pot that stood on the window. I entered, and
called for a dram and some meat. The dram was understood,
and a half-mutchkin of good whisky brought to me (they do not
deal in gills hereabouts), but no meat. I understood that the
master and mistress were both absent at some place of worship,
as no one ever appeared to me but two girls, who were visibly
menials. I again called, and ordered some meat. A girl
answered me in Gaelic, and I her in English, for a good while
without either of us being the wiser. I then made signs to let
her know that I wanted meat, taking care to give the whisky a
push that she might not think that I wanted some more of it ;
but, in spite of my teeth, I was misconstrued, and another half-
mutchkin of whisky clapped down to me in another pot. I
expostulated a great deal ; to no purpose. The girls came both
into the room, and being tickled by our embarrassment, opened
the flood-gates of their mirth, giggling and laughing aloud. I
was inflamed by one of those sudden bursts of passion which
sometimes, although not very frequently, quite overcome my
reason, springing up in a rage, and, swearing like a trooper, I laid
hold of them violently, and turned first the one, and then the
other, out of the room, and closing the door behind them with a
force as if I wished to throw down the house ; while the poor
creatures were so affrighted that their limbs almost refused their

office of furthering their escape, the girls thinking, I daresay, that they were attacked, and their master's house taken up by a ruffian.

I threw myself again into my seat over my whisky, where in less than a minute I began to repent most heartily of my folly. Never did I yet suffer myself to get into a rage but the reflection cost me dear.

I would willingly have tarried a night hereabout, thinking it a country about the state of which it was worth my while to make some inquiry; but judging it impossible to lodge here, I again called *ben* one of the maids, who entered with great caution, and with the most timid air imaginable. I assumed as mild a demeanour as I was able, offering her what money she thought proper to accept of. Seeing one of the stoups untouched, she charged sixpence.

I again took to my road. I began to grow very impatient, knowing that it would infallibly lead me into the country where I had been last year, and at length, seeing a small, winding, path ascending the mountains to the northward, I took to it without hesitation. But as my letters are always growing longer I will leave off.

J. H.

DEAR SIR,—I took an abrupt leave of you in my last, while climbing the mountains and just about to take my last look of the country of Loch Carron.

I must here explain a circumstance to you which I believe I have never done yet, and which I ought to have done long ago, that is, what is meant by *a country* in the Highlands. In all the inland glens the boundaries of a country are invariably marked out by the skirts of the visible horizon as viewed from the bottom of the valley. All beyond that is denominated *another country*, and is called by another name. It is thus that the Highland countries are almost innumerable. But on the western coast, which is all indented by extensive arms of the sea, and where the countries that are not really islands, are peninsulas, the above usage is varied, and the bounds of the country marked out by the sea coast. Along the whole of the shores of Argyll and Inverness shires, this latter is the division, but as soon as you enter Rossshire, the former is again adopted. Thus the country of Kintail, the country of Loch Carron, the country of Torridon, the two straths of Loch Broom, etc., comprehend both sides of their respective firths, with all the waters that descend into them.

Shortly after I lost sight of the valley my path divided into twain, equally well frequented. I hesitated long which to take, having no directions saving what I had from the map, but following the left hand one it led me at length into the Vale of Colan, a curious, sequestered place, in the midst of the mountains to the east of Sir Hector Mackenzie's forest. The haughs are of considerable extent, of a deep sandy soil, with a clear stream winding through them ; and some of the haughs were very good for such a country. The hills around it were very black, and mostly covered with strong heather.

I spoke to no person here, nor all this way, but again took to the muir, being resolved if possible to reach the house of Letterewe that night, but ere I got into the next valley I was quite exhausted by hunger and fatigue, having travelled an unconscionable length of way, and a slated house appearing on a plain beyond the river I made toward it.

I was obliged to wade through the river once, which being in a swelled state was very deep, and getting to the house asked if it was an inn, and was answered in the affirmative, at which I was very well satisfied. At this place I lodged. It is called Kinloch-ewe; was built by Sir Hector Mackenzie, in order to accommodate himself and others travelling from Dingwall into his country of Gairloch, or toward the ferry of Poolewe, where there is a packet once each week to Lewis, and though he hath annexed several advantages to it, it is very ill kept and in very bad order. He had only a few days preceding that, lodged there himself, and had certainly little reason to be pleased with his accommodation. The floor was well sanded as is the custom in that country. The windows were broken, and the bed was as hard as a stone. They had however plenty of whisky, oat-meal cakes, tea, and sugar, with some eggs, and stinking fish, on which I fared sumptuously.

I spent the following forenoon in the company of a Mr. Mackenzie, a farmer in a glen above that.   He conducted me along a part of the road to Letterewe, and showed me the old

K

burying ground of Ellon Mare, on the gravestones of which no name nor epitaph is to be seen, saving one or two rude figures and some initials.

I at length arrived at the house of Letterewe, and was received by Mr. M'Intyre (to whom I was recommended by a friend) with much kindness without any ceremony. This was exactly a man for my purpose. He had been from his youth an extensive dealer, both in cattle and sheep, and had travelled over the whole Highlands and Western Islands, and now in company with some English gentlemen farms an extraordinary extent of land, consisting of the whole estates of Letterewe and Strathnashalloch, the former belonging to Mr. Mackenzie, to whose sister he is married, and the other to Mr. Davidson.

He hath a handsome house and offices, which he, however, is going to enlarge, and having discovered large veins of white marble up in the linns of a rivulet near the house, he burneth it into lime, using it both for building and manure, and manageth the croft lying around his house in a manner which would not disgrace the banks of the Forth. There were to be seen shotts of turnips and potatoes, in drills as straight as a line, and in a forward state of vegetation, and clover and rye-grass so strong that it was beginning to lodge on the ground. The vigilance of this man is remarkable. This piece of land was one continued cairn of stones. Also the attention he pays to every department of his numerous flocks and shepherds is the most exact and constant, and he hath, by his vigilance and attention raised himself, from nothing, to affluence and credit.   I had often heard of the man before I saw him.   He was known on all the northern roads and markets by the appellation of *little Mackintyre*, he being low of stature, but as mettled at climbing among the rocks as the foxes—his greatest enemies.

As I am not in an humour for writing to-day, I shall close this letter with an anecdote of him which I had often heard told by Mr. James Welch.

The Hon. Lord Macdonald once at a market recognised the cattle from his farms in M'Intyre's possession, and began enquiring where he got them, who he got them from, etc.   He informed his lordship in an indifferent manner, that he got them from Lord Macdonald's factor in Skye.   But when the other began enquiring about the prices, and expenses, M'Intyre ignorant of who he was took him off so sharply that he knew not what to say excusing his curiosity, when a gentleman accompanying him introduced them to one another by their names.   M'Intyre started, and with great quickness whipped off his bonnet, threw it on the ground, and placed his foot upon it, making an apology which pleased his lordship so much that he shook him by the hand, declaring that he was no stranger to his honesty, and adding, that the M'Intyres and the Macdonalds were the same people.

I am, yours for ever,

J. H.

DEAR SIR,—I had conducted you in idea as far as Letterewe on the north-east bank of Loch Maree, and given you some hints of improvements commenced there by the farmer, which are only rendered remarkable by reflecting on the situation of the place.

It is, as I said, on the side of Loch Maree, by which there is access in boats from all corners of the lake, but it is everywhere else surrounded by shaggy cliffs, and bold, projecting promontories, washed around the bottom by the lake, and rising to the height of from one to four hundred yards, in an almost perpendicular direction.   It is thus rendered inaccessible to the most expert foot passenger without a guide, and entirely so to horses, unless some passage is explored through amongst the mountains, that I never saw.

I proposed going to Ardlair next day, but was detained by the importunities of Mr. Mackintyre until the morning of the third day.   He showed me everything in the vicinity that was worth seeing, and seemed much attached to me, being seldom visited by any from so distant a country.

There was another traveller wind-bound here, of a different description.   This was Miss Jane Downie, sister to Mr. Downie, whose house I had lately left, who, from her father's house at the Manse of Urray, in the vicinity of Dingwall, was on a journey to the island of Lewis, to see some relations.   Being daughter to a respectable clergyman, she had received a genteel education, a circumstance to which the utmost attention is paid by all families of rank in the north.   To this she added an extensive knowledge of the world, of which she had seen a considerable part for one of her age and sex, for besides her acquaintance with both the Highlands and Lowlands, she had resided some years at St. Petersburgh with a sister, who was there distinguished by royal favour and protection.

It was this young lady who first inspired me with the resolution of visiting the remote country of the Lewis, by describing it to me as the scene of the most original and hereditary modes and customs that were anywhere to be met with in the British Isles, and I repented an hundred times that I ever parted company with her before we reached Stornoway, to which port she was going, straight.

On Wednesday we breakfasted early, and set off for Ardlair in Mr. Mackintyre's boat, who still insisted on our staying, assuring me that we would find much difficulty in our passage, if it was at all possible, the wind being so strong, and straight ahead. We had not proceeded far on the lake before we found this verified, and after rowing stoutly for about an hour, in which time we had not advanced a mile and a half, they put the boat ashore on the lee side of a point, declaring that it was impossible to proceed farther.

We were now much worse than if we had set off on foot from Letterewe. However, taking two men with us as guides, we *set a stout heart to a strait brae*, and explored a crooked way amongst the rocks; continuing for a long space to climb the hill in quite a contrary direction from the place we were bound to.

Our guides then led us over rocks and precipices, which on looking at I thought a goat could not have kept its feet on, and had it not been owing to the nature of the stones, the surface of which was rough and crusty, it was impossible that we could have effected an escape, especially on such a day. I was in the greatest distress on account of the lady. The wind which had grown extremely rough took such impression on her clothes, that I was really apprehensive that it would carry her off, and looked back several times with terror for fear that I should see her flying headlong toward the lake like a swan.

It was however a scene worthy of these regions, to see a lady of a most delicate form and elegantly dressed, in such a situation, climbing over the dizzy precipices in a retrograde direction, and after fixing one foot, hanging by both hands until she could find a small hold for the other. What would the most of your Edinburgh ladies have done here, my dear sir? I believe if the wind had not changed they might have stayed with little Mackintyre altogether, for they could not have passed over these rocks.

Miss Downie's clothes were partly torn and otherwise abused, and the wind carried off her kerchief altogether. For upwards of a mile we were forced to scramble in this manner, making use of all fours, and in one place I was myself afraid of growing giddy, and durst not turn my eyes toward the lake so far below my feet. We, however, arrived safe at Ardlair at one o'clock, p.m., having been *five hours* on our passage, which in distance would not measure as many English miles, and were received by the Messrs. Mackenzie with great politeness and attention, and we soon became extremely happy, and though we did not forget, laughed most heartily at our late perilous situation.

The weather growing more moderate toward the evening we made a most agreeable excursion round several óf the principal island of Loch Maree in a handsome boat with a sail. These islands have a much more bare appearance than they exhibited some years ago, the ancient woods with which they were covered being either entirely cut down and removed, or most miserably thinned.　One island on which there are some remains of a temporary residence is covered with wood and rich verdure.　We landed on several of them and carried off numbers of eggs from the nests of the gulls, thousands of which were hovering and screaming around us.　The Holy Island was so far to the lee-ward that we could not visit it that night for fear we should not get back.

I was truly delighted with the view from these islands, although it consisted much more of the sublime than of the beauti-ful.　The old high house of Ardlair faced us from a romantic little elevated plain, bounded on the north with a long ridge of perpendicular rock of a brown colour, and the low islands on which we stood were finely contrasted with the precipitous shores already mentioned, on the one side, and the mountains of Sir Hector Mackenzie's forest on the other, whose pointed tops bored the firmament, and appeared of a colour as white as the finest marble.

I was greatly pleased with the Mackenzies, as well as with the old lady of Letterewe, their mother, (the gentlemen present being brethren to the proprietor,) and began to think that the farther north I proceeded I was still going to find the people more intelligent, and possessing qualities more and more estimable. As I had a line of introduction to Mr. John, the youngest, from a friend in Edinburgh, he furnished me with one to an acquaintance in the Lewis.

Next morning we arose and departed. Mr. Alexander Mackenzie of Auchnasheen (towards Woodrigill), one of his farms on which his family resides, and Mr. John and I, again entered the boat, and having a fair wind we skipped along the surface of Loch Maree with great velocity. We landed on St. Mary's Isle, and I had the superstition to go and drink of the holy well so renowned in that country among the vulgar and superstitious, like me, for the cure of insanity in all its stages, and so well authenticated are the facts, the most stubborn of all proofs, that even people of the most polite and modern ways of thinking, are obliged to allow of its efficacy in some instances. But as mine was only an attack of poetical hydrophobia, including my tendency to knight errantry, which however ridiculous to some, I take pleasure in. I omitted, however, the appendage of the ceremony, which in all probability is the most necessary and efficacious branch of it, namely, that of being plunged over head and ears three times in the lake.

But although I write thus lightly to you of the subject, I

acknowledge that I felt a kind of awe on my mind on wandering over the burying-ground and ruins of the Virgin's chapel, held in such veneration by the devout, though illiterate fathers of the present generation.   This I mentioned to Mr. Mackenzie, who assured me that had I visited it before the wood was cut down, such was the effect, that it would have been impossible not to be struck with a religious awe.

Shortly after we arrived again at Letterewe, where I took leave of you in my last, and where your fancy must leave me for a few days, until my next arrival, when it shall conduct you through a scene the most awful that has yet been visited.

I remain, sir, your most affectionate servant,

J. H.

———

DEAR SIR,—Leaving the banks of Loch Maree, I mounted the hills of Letterewe, accompanied by Mackintyre and Mackenzie, who, perceiving that my attention was much taken by the uncouth scenery, promised that they would lead me through some which I should not see equalled in Scotland, and I believe they were as good as their word, the whole scenery in some parts of Letterewe estate being dreadful and grand beyond measure; and here, as in places of that nature throughout the Highlands, the principal parts were named after some of the Fingalian heroes.   The lake is named after the chief, being denominated Loch Fion, or the Fion Loch.

L

To enumerate particularly the different appearances of each tremendous precipice that interlards this truly terrific scene is impossible. I neither have time nor words suited to the description, but I cannot avoid taking notice of the black rock, or Craig-tullich; for although any other of these views may be matched in the country, yet this one is certainly not only unequalled, but far out of reach of comparison. It extends a whole English mile in length, along all which extent there is not a passage where a creature could pass, and it is so appropriately termed black that it appears wholly stained with ink, and its dreadful face, all of which can be seen from one view, everywhere distorted by dark slits, gaping and yawning chasms, with every feature of a most awful deformity, conveying to the attentive spectator ideas of horror which could scarcely be excelled by a glimpse of hell itself !

Should a merry companion choose, in order to enjoy the sight of the most profound and exquisite tumble, to give you an unmannerly push from the top of it, you might descend for nearly half a mile in the most straight line towards the centre of gravity. You might indeed happen to leave a rag of your coat on the point of one cliff, or a shoe, or your brains perhaps on another, but these are trifling circumstances. The worst thing attending it would be, that the pleasure arising from a view of your gracefully alighting would be entirely lost from the top, as you would appear of no greater magnitude than a forked bulrush. Remember that it is to your fancy that I am addressing myself, my dear sir. I always wish you to see everything nearly the same as I did.

At a great distance he showed me a large perpendicular rock, with the entrance to a cavern near the bottom. In this dismal hole, in the midst of this huge wilderness, wonderful to relate, a widow and her family hath resided many years! When she first took possession of this dreary abode her youngest son was a sucking infant. Yet she was obliged to cross the mountains once a week to seek milk and other articles of food; while owing to their being so inaccessible she was unable to carry her child along with her, and was obliged to put out the fire and leave him to shift for himself. He had by such lodging and treatment acquired a weakness in his back, and it was feared he would never overcome it, as he still could not walk, but only creep, though I think they said he was six or seven years of age.

Mr. Mackenzie told me that he was once passing that way with an English gentleman, on business in that country, and observing no smoke, he suspected the woman to be from home, so without mentioning anything of the matter to his companion he led him to take a view of the cavern. The gentleman was almost out of his wits when he saw a creature bearing such a resemblance to the human form, come crawling towards him from the interior of the cavern. Alas! my dear Sir, one half of the world knows little how the other half lives. ' Nor how they die either, James,' you will add when you read the following.

In a deep sequestered hollow among these rocks, my friend

showed us a shealing far beneath our feet, where a man and his wife lately came to reside during the summer months with their cattle and goats. The woman fell a travailling in childbirth, and for want of assistance, which was impossible there to be procured, there she died and was buried.

From a precipice near to this we had a view of a curious bason of very romantic dimensions, but in order to see it properly we were obliged to lie down full length on our breasts, and make long necks over the verge. I was afraid to trust my head, and ordered Mr. Mackenzie to keep a firm hold of the tails of my coat, but before I could reach so far as to have a proper survey, I was obliged to roar out to be pulled back, my ' conscience having failed me,' as I once heard a boy say in the same predicament.

We proceeded on in company through a large track of this rough country, and were often so immersed among rocks, that I saw no possibility of escaping, but Mackintyre was so well acquainted with the gaps that he always found an open door, as he termed it. Nor did they ever leave me until they landed me in one of the glens of Strathinashalloch, having conducted me full ten miles, and I took leave of them deeply impressed with their kindness and attention. I shall have occasion to take notice of some intelligence received from Mackintyre afterwards.

I now proceeded down a glen several miles in length, which brought me into the Valley of Strathinashalloch, near the head of the lake of that name. The valley is now inhabited only by

Mr. Macintyre's shepherds, but there were considerable crops of corn and potatoes left by the tenants who had removed last term. It is of considerable extent, and there is good fishing in the river and loch, which is entirely free.   This estate is now the property of Mr. Davidson, and though there are some more detached parts arable, and possessed by the natives, the greatest extent is now farmed by Mr. Macintyre, at the trifling rent of £200; and I am certain, if things continue at present prices, that he may have a clear return of £600 or £700 a year from it, if once he had a proper stock on it, which he had not when I saw it, having only entered at Whitsunday.

He showed me the boundary on one side, and his shepherd the same on the other, and I could not compute that part held by him alone at less than 15,000 acres, all of which is well mixed, good Highland ground, most of it accessible, not being nearly so rough as Letterewe; free of lying stones, and tolerably well sheltered.   What an excellent bargain at such a time!

The truth is, there are several low-country gentlemen getting into excellent bargains by their buying lands in that country, of which Mr. Davidson and Mr. Innes are instances; and I cannot help having a desperate ill-will at them on that score.   I cannot endure to hear of a Highland chieftain selling his patrimonial property, the cause of which misfortune I always attribute to the goodness of his heart, and the liberality of his sentiments; unwilling to drive off the people who have so long looked to him as their protector, yet whose system of farming cannot furnish them with the means of paying him one-fourth, and in some situations not more than a tenth of the value of his land; and as unwilling to let fall the dignity of his house, and the consequence amongst his friends, which his fathers maintained. Is not his case particularly hard, my dear sir? All things are doubled and tripled in their value, save his lands. His family—his retainers —his public burdens! These last being regulated by the old valuation, lie very hard upon him, and all must be scraped up among the poor, meagre tenants, in twos and threes of *silly* lambs, hens, and pounds of butter.

I shall follow the idea no farther else I shall run mad, but as the value of these hills is every year more and more conspicuous, I anticipate with joy the approaching period when the stigmas of poverty and pride so liberally bestowed on the highlanders by our south-country gentry will be as inapplicable to the inhabitants of that country as of any in the island. Their riches are increasing, and will increase much more, and when that shall be the case they will require no pride, as that has mostly consisted in maintaining the appearance of a rank to which in reality their circumstances were quite inadequate.

After going over another track of bare rocky land I descended the beautiful strath of little Loch Broom, and before sunset arrived at the house of Dundonnel, the seat of George Mackenzie Esquire, of Dundonnel.

I am, yours, etc.,

J. H.

DEAR SIR,—I was received by Dundonnel at the head of the green before the house, he having, it seems, eyed my approach from one of the windows, and he welcomed and introduced me to his family with a respectful attention and ceremony which greatly distressed me; and notwithstanding every endeavour at a more unreserved familiarity, it rather increased than diminished during my stay. Every time that I entered the room, the whole family, small and great, must be on their feet to receive me, so that in spite of Dundonnel's good humour, and he is a remarkably cheerful and unassuming man, I was in no wise easy, on account of the stir that I occasioned in the family, and the rich meals that were provided.

He hath one master for instructing his family in the languages, and arithmetic; and another for teaching them music and dancing. We had thus plenty of music at night, having always three fiddles in tune; and every one bore a hand at swelling the lively concert, where the Highland strathspeys and reels were the prevailing strains. They were pleased to applaud my performance, which caused me to saw away as if I had it by the piece.

We always remained at the punch-bowl until the blackbird sung at the window, as this was Dundonnel's rule, which custom he would not dispense with. We spent a day in viewing the strath, and to have a better general view of the estate Mr. George and I climbed to the top of a hill on the ridge betwixt the two Loch-Brooms. It extends fully eighteen Scotch miles from east to west, and may be about ten miles broad, at an average, but on the south it is terribly interwoven with Mr. Davidson's ground. It is an excellent pastoral estate, and the vale of the little strath is pleasant and fertile. It hath plenty of natural wood in its upper parts, and the laird hath beautified the vicinity of his mansion-house with extensive plantations, which are in a thriving state.

Most of the reflections in my last may be applied to Dundonnel. His glens are so crammed full of stout, able-bodied men and women, that the estate under the present system must have enough to do maintaining them. The valleys are impoverished by perpetual cropping, and saving one farm on the north-east quarter, held by the Messrs. Mitchell, the extensive mountains are all waste; for the small parcels of diminutive sheep which the natives have, are all herded below nearest the dwellings, and are housed every night. Dundonnel asked me what I thought it would bring annually if let off in sheep walks. I said I had only had a superficial view of it, but that, exclusive of a reasonable extent near the house, to be occupied by himself, it would bring not below £2,000. He said his people would never pay him the half of that. He was loath to chase them all away to America, but at present they did not pay him above £700. He hath, however, the pleasure of absolute sway. He is even more so in his domains than Bonaparte is in France. I saw him call two men from their labour a full mile, to carry us through the water. I told him he must not expect to be served thus by the shepherds if once he had given them possession.

I now understand on enquiry that I must either relinquish my visit to the Lewis, or to Sutherland, for that there was no possibility of obtaining a passage. After leaving Ullapool, and learning on the third day after my arrival at Dundonnel, that the *Isabella* of Stornoway had been taking in a load of stones on the south shore of Loch Broom, and was only waiting the arrival of one of the crew from the country, to set sail for that port, I took leave of Dundonnel, and set off in order to procure a passage by that vessel. I reached the place by two o'clock, but owing to a contrary wind, and the flow of the tide, they could not sail that night. I knew not what to do then. The crew were out of provisions, and there were none to be had in that place. There was a whole village of Highland cottages hard by, but when the sailors, who could talk Gaelic, could procure no provisions, by what means was I, who had no Gaelic, to support myself! As I was under the necessity of trying what could be done I went to all the houses, but could not get one word of English. There was, it seems, only one man amongst them who made the smallest pretensions towards it, and he being gone a little from home, some of them had the goodness to fetch him. He was the worst talker of English that I ever heard attempt it. It was down-right nonsense, a mixture which no man could comprehend. He took me to his little hovel, and gave me whey to drink, but he had no bread until he baked it, which he made shift to do in the most unfeasible manner imaginable.

On parting with Dundonnel he said that if I wanted to be

M

well treated on my passage to the Lewis, or yet to be welcome
when I got there, I must necessarily pretend to want either
horses or cows. I made some objections which he quite over-
ruled, and I promised to obey ; and on this man asking what I
was wanting in that country I told him I wanted horses.
Unluckily for me the man had horses to sell, and led me many
miles out to the hills to look at them, and I could not get quit of
buying them on any account until I had to promise to come
back that way and buy all the horses in the country, and on that
day twenty days he was to have all the horses in the strath
collected. I was heartily tired of Dundonnel's plan, and fully
convinced of the justness of the old proverb, 'truth tells aye
best.' I never more in the course of my journey had recourse
to equivocation. The man had no one in the house with him
saving a child of four years old. I asked 'What was become of
his wife?' His answer was, 'He pe con see hir muter; he pe
shild lenoch after her.' There were some of his horses which he
denominated *girrons*, others were *pullocks*, and some were *no
pullocks*. He had no milk in his house, only some sour whey,
the cows being out on the hills at the shealings. He made
sowens to our supper, but as he did not use the necessary
precaution to shill, or strain them, they were unconsciously rough
with seeds.

I now began to look about me where I should sleep, but he did
not long suffer me to remain in suspense, for bringing in a large
arm-full of green heather, he flung it down by the side of the

wall, then strewing a few rushes over it, he spread one pair of
clean blankets over it, and there was my bed.   I found fault
with nothing, but stripping to the skin, I wrapped myself first in
my shepherd's plaid, and then covered me with his blanket.   I
made shift to pass the night, although not very agreeably, for, as
the tops of the heather depressed, the stubborn roots found
means more and more to annoy my shoulders and ribs, and so
audacious were some of them that they penetrated Donald's white
blanket, and I left them so firmly connected, that I am sure on
his removing the blanket, a good many of the roots would adhere
to it.

Next morning I went on board the sloop, and about seven o'clock
A.M., we heaved anchor and got under way, but as the small breeze
that was blowing was straight ahead of the vessel, we beat up
the whole day without getting out of the loch, sometimes among
the Summer Isles, and sometimes hard off the shore opposite
them, to the south, and at the close of the day we found ourselves
immediately off a rocky point betwixt the channel and the broad
loch.   Here the boat was sent ashore to bring a lady on board,
who was bound to Stornoway.   She was not ready, and the
master of the vessel was obliged to wait on her, she being mother
of the owner.   There being no anchorage nigh, he was forced to
lie to in the entrance all night, in the worst humour that possibly
could be, cursing the whole sex, and wishing them all wind-
bound for a season, and especially the old, weather beaten hulk,

who caused him to endanger so good a vessel off the face of a rock, while the wind was sunk and the tide so violent.

As the sea was heavy in the mouth of the bay, the vessel wrought incessantly during the whole night. I became very uneasy, but knowing nothing of the nature of the sea fever, I thought I was attacked by the influenza, but how was I vexed next morning at having suffered such a night, when I was shown the house of Woodrigill, at the end of a bay not an hour's walking distant, where I could have lodged with the kind Achnasheen.

I remain, your most obedient,

J. H.

———

Sir,—I took leave of you in my last while lying on board, sick of the influenza; but having got no meat for a whole natural day, saving a small piece of cake and a little old cheese, I was becoming extremely hungry, and desired two of the crew to row me ashore. I went to the house of Melton, and took a hearty breakfast with Mrs. Morrison, who immediately after accompanied me to the vessel, and we began to steer onward, but the breeze continuing straight ahead, it was near noon before we got into the open channel.

As soon as we got clear of the Summer Isles, the tide then turning to the north, we took a long stretch in the same direction, passed the Summer Isles, doubled the point of Coygarch, and the day being fair and clear, got an excellent view of the mountains of that country.   They had a verdant appearance, but a passenger assured me that the fine weather made them appear so, for that they were nevertheless mostly covered with a mossy surface.

Still holding on in the same direction, and having an excellent spy-glass on board, we got a view of the shores of Loch Eynard; and passing the Rhu of Assynt, although then at a considerable distance out on the channel, a prodigious range of the rugged mountains on Lord Reay's country presented itself to view, forming the most striking and perforated outline I had yet seen. I was afterwards convinced that the extraordinary appearance which they exhibited had been occasioned in part by some small skiffs of mist which had been hovering about their summits, and which I had taken for the horizon beyond them, these causing them to appear as if bored through in many places.

Our skipper steered thus far to the north in hopes that the breeze would drop into the north-east before evening.   In this, however, he was disappointed, and the tide turning to the south, he tacked about, steering to the south-west, or a little to the west, and a little before sunset the breeze sunk entirely, and there was not a breath.   My patience now took its leave of me for some time altogether.   Although I was never actually sick, yet I found myself growing squeamish and uneasy, forsaken by the breeze in the very midst of a broad channel, and, for anything that I knew, condemned to hobble on that unstable element for a week, or perhaps much longer.

Mrs. Morison, who is well versed in naval affairs, and has been frequently known to take the helm into her own hand in dangers, perceiving my face growing long, gave me a dram, and expressed her surprise that I was no worse, having never been at sea before, assuring me that a calm was worse to endure than a gale.

As the sails continued all set, waiting to take advantage of the first breeze, and as they flapped and wrought in conjunction with the waves, the ship rolled exceedingly at times. I, who imputed no part of it to the rigging, could not forbear, in my then desperate condition, from expressing, with great bitterness and folly, my indignation at the malevolence of the sea, that would not be still and at peace, when nothing was troubling it, asking the sailors 'What was putting it astir now when there was not a breath? It was certainly an earthquake.' There was, however, one comfort. We were in no danger now of perishing for hunger, Mrs. Morison having brought plenty on board from her farm. During the first day, when cruising in Loch Broom, the master and I were forced to content ourselves with a fardle cake between us, and a piece of old cheese, the sailors regaling themselves with some crabbed shell-fish and sea-weeds, which they had scraped from the rocks on shore. Highlandmen are not nice of their diet. But now we had plenty of tea, sugar, eggs, cakes, and fish.

My chagrin was somewhat diverted near the fall of evening by contemplating the extensive prospect. We were becalmed exactly in the middle of the channel which separates Lewis from the mainland, and the evening being remarkably fine and clear we could see distinctly the Isle of Skye, the Shant Isles, the Lewis, and all that range of mountains in Ross-shire and Sutherland, stretching from Torridon to Cape Wrath. By reason of their distance they now appeared low. The sea, though in its natural perturbed state, being unruffled by the smallest breeze appeared an ocean of heaving crystal, of different colors in different directions, presenting alternately spots of the deepest green, topaz, and purple ; for which I could not in the least account by any appearance in the sky, which was all of one colour.

Such a scene, so entirely new to me could not fail of attracting my attention, which it did to such a degree that I remained on deck all night. The light of the moon at length prevailed. She hovered low above the Shant Isles, and shed a stream of light on the glassy surface of the sea, in the form of a tall crescent, of such lustre that it dazzled the sight. The whole scene tended to inspire the mind with serenity and awe, and in the contemplation of it I composed a few verses addressed to the Deity, which I will give you bye and bye, and if you apprehend that they move a little more heavily than my verses were wont to do, remember that they are *sea-sick*.

VERSES ADDRESSED TO THE DEITY.

Great source of perfection, and pole of devotion !
Thy presence surrounds me wherever I roam ;

I see Thee as well in the wild heaving ocean
  As in the most sacred magnificent dome.
While viewing this scene with amazement and wonder,
  I see Thee in yonder moon's watery gleam.
Thy voice I have heard from the cloud burst in thunder ;
  Now hear it from wild fowls which over me scream;
Oh ! teach me to fear, to adore, and to love Thee
  As Sovereign of earth and those heavens I see.
But oh ! above all, with warm gratitude move me
  For all Thy great mercies bestow'd upon me,
In all my lone wand'rings, oh guide and direct me,
  As round the bleak shores of the Hebrides I roam,
From evils and dangers defend and protect me,
  And lead me in peace to my sweet native home.
And when my life's wearisome journey is ended,
  May I, in Thy presence, those heavens survey,
So sanded with suns ! amid seraphs so splendid
  To sing, where no night shall encroach on the day.

'Ay James; I never saw you in so serious a mood as this before.' ' 'Tis no matter my dear sir; I am very often in such a mood, but it never continues long at a time, and I forgot to inform you that it was the evening of the Sabbath.'

During all this time, although we varied our position greatly to the North, and South, with the tides, we were quite stationary as to proceeding in our course, the vessel floating with her stern towards Stornoway. I wished myself fairly on terra firma again; I cared not on which side of the channel.

Early in the morning, all being quiet, I had wrapped myself in my shepherd's plaid, and was stretched among some cables on deck, busied in perusing Shakespeare's monstrous tragedy of 'Titus

Andronicus,' and just when my feelings were wrought to the highest pitch of horror, I was alarmed by an uncommon noise, as of something bursting, and which I apprehended was straight over me, when starting up with great emotion, I was almost blinded by a shower of brine.   But how was I petrified with amazement at seeing a huge monster, in size like a horse, sinking into the sea by the side of the vessel, something after the manner of a rope tumbler, and so near me that I could have struck him with a spear.   I bawled out to the crew to be upon the alert, for that here was a *monstrous whale* going to *coup* the ship, and seizing the boat-hook was going, as I thought, to maul him most terribly. He had rather got out of my reach, and one of the crew took it from me for fear I should lose it, assuring me that I could not pierce him although it was sharp, which it was not.

After the sun rose, the sails began to fill, and we moved on almost imperceptibly towards Stornoway.   The whale kept by the vessel the whole morning, sometimes on one side, sometimes on the other.   Being always immoderately addicted to fishing, I was in the highest degree interested.   I was also impatient at such a huge fish being so near me.   He was exactly the length of the vessel, a sloop, if I mistake not, about seventy or eighty tons.   I once called to one of the sailors to come and see how he rubbed sides with the ship.   'Eh ! said he, ' he pe wanting one of us to breakfast with him !'

Your most obedient,

J. H.

Dear Sir,—We at length entered the harbour of Stornoway, and about seven o'clock in the evening cast anchor within a very short space of the houses, having been exactly sixty hours on the passage, a distance of scarcely so many miles.

As soon as I arrived, I went to the head inn, held by Mr. Creighton, a silly, despicable man, but privileged in having an excellent wife. During the whole of that evening I could not walk without taking hold of everything that came in my way, impressed with an idea that all things were in motion. I was very unfortunate in not meeting with the people to whom I was recommended here. I had a letter for Mr. Chapman at Seaforth Lodge, but he was absent in Uig, parting some land, and Mrs. Chapman being in a poor state of health, I never presented myself. I had a letter to Mr. Donald Macdonald, and another to Mr. Robertson, both of Stornoway, and in whose company I spent some time ; but the one was obliged to go from home in the packet, and the other did not come home until the last day that I was there.

I wandered about the town and neighbouring country for there days, sometimes in company with one, and sometimes with another. There was a Captain Marshal, from the neighbourhood of Fochabers, lodging in the same house with me, a sober, sensible man, with whom I was very happy.

I was indeed greatly surprised at meeting with such a large and populous town in such a remote and distant country. It was but the preceding week that I ever heard of it, and yet it is quite

unrivalled in all the west of Scotland north of the Clyde, either
in population, trade, or commerce.   I was informed by Mr.
Robison, comptroller of the Customs, that, according to the last
survey, which was then newly taken, the town and suburbs con-
tained nearly seventeen hundred souls.   Mr. Macdonald, to whom
I mentioned this, doubted its containing so many, but was certain
that there were above a thousand.

There is one full half of the town composed of as elegant
houses, with even more genteel inhabitants, than are generally
to be met with in the towns of North Britain which depend
solely on the fishing and trade.   The principal and modern part
of the town stands on a small point of land stretching into the
harbour in the form of a T, and as you advance back from the
shore the houses grow gradually worse.   The poor people have a
part by themselves, on a rising ground to the north-east of the
town, and though all composed of the meanest huts it is laid out
in streets and rows as regularly as a camp.   The houses on the
shore to the eastward and those at the head of the bay are of
the medium sort.   It hath an excellent harbour, and is much
ornamented by the vicinity of Seaforth Lodge, which stands on a
rising ground overlooking the town and harbour.   The town is
much incommoded by the want of streets or pavements.   Even
the most elegant houses facing the harbour, saving a small road
close by the wall, have only the rough sea shore to pass and
repass on, which being composed of rough stones, which fly from

the foot, grinding on one another, forms a most uncomfortable footpath.

As the peculiárities observable in the modes and customs of the inhabitants are applicable to the whole island, I shall note a few of them on taking leave of it. I shall only observe here, that the well directed and attended schools, the enlightened heads, and enlarged ideas of a great number of the people of Stornoway bid fair to sow the seeds of emulation, and consequently of improvement in that remote country. It is a general complaint through all the Long Island that the poorer sort are much addicted to pilfering. I persuaded myself that I saw a striking evidence to the contrary in the inhabitants of this town. During the daytime there were thousands of white fish spread on the shores, drying on the sand. When night came they were gathered and built up in large heaps, and loosely covered with some coarse cloth, and when the sun grew warm next day were again spread. Now, my dear Sir, I'll wager you durst not have exposed your fish in such a manner at Edinburgh, for as fine a place as it is.

Although the island is not noted for riots, I had no very favourable specimen of their absolute command over their passions. On the very night of my arrival a desperate affray took place in the room adjoining to that in which I slept. Several respectable men, the collector, and one of the bailiffs, were engaged in it. It was fought with great spirit and monstrous vociferation. Desperate wounds were given and received, the door was split in pieces, and twice some of the party entered my chamber. I was overpowered with sleep, having got none at sea, and minded them very little, but was informed of all by Mr. Marshall. A ship's captain, in particular, wrought terrible devastation. He ran foul of the table, although considerably to the windward, which he rendered a perfect wreck, sending all its precious cargo of crystal, china, etc., to the bottom, and attacked his opponents with such fury and resolution that he soon laid most of them sprawling on the deck. Some of the combatants being next day confined to their beds, summonses were issued, and a prosecution commenced, but the parties being very nearly connected a treaty was set on foot, and the preliminaries signed before I left Stornoway.

On the evening preceding my departure I hired a lad to accompany me round the island for eighteen pence per day, on condition that he was not to go off Lewis. At Creighton's the entertainment was as good as could be expected, for although they have neither brewer, baker, nor barber in the town, professionally, yet every man privileged with a beard is a barber, and every woman unencumbered with a family is a baker, and I suppose Mrs. Creighton is none of the most inferior practitioners, as we got very good wheaten loaves, though not exactly conformable in shape to those used in our country. Our breakfasts were thus rendered as comfortable as they are anywhere, and though at dinners and suppers we had seldom any beef or mutton, we had great abundance, as well as variety, of fish, fowls, and eggs. I expected my bill to run high, but how was I surprised on calling for it to see that I was charged no more than sixpence for each meal. I was agreeably deceived, and observed to my hostess that a man might eat himself rich here and fat at the same time. 'A very poor specimen of your wit, James!'

Thus being furnished with several letters, some whisky, biscuit, and a full half of a Lewis cheese, as hard as wood, Malcolm and I set out in the morning, and taking the only road in the whole island, proceeded northward through a dreary waste, without ever being blest with the sight of a human habi-tation, or a spot where it was possible to live upon, there being only one extensive morass the whole way. We passed a flock of native sheep, which was the greatest curiosity I had ever seen. I saw a man coming with hasty strides to waylay us. As I suspected that he would have no English I never regarded him, although he had got within speech as I passed, but Malcolm, who carried considerable weight, being fallen quite behind, he inter-cepted, and testified his regret that I had passed him, as he meant to treat us at his shealing.

Our road, after carrying us straight on for ten miles, like several of the Highland roads, left us all at once in the midst of a trackless morass, through which it had been cut at the deepness of several yards. The plan in making roads being mostly to clear the channel of whatever incumbrances choke it up. Malcolm being now fallen at least a mile back I scorned to wait, but holding on in the same direction I soon discovered the northern ocean, and the manse of Barvas facing me at some distance, to which I bent my course, and reached it just as the family were rising from breakfast. I produced my letter of introduction, which the minister read, but declared it perfectly superfluous, for that my appearance was a sufficient introduction. I knew that this was to let me know how welcome a stranger was in that country, for alas! I knew that my appearance commanded no great respect. I was only dressed as a shepherd when I left Ettrick, and my dress was now become very shabby, and I often wondered at the attention shown to me.

The Reverend Mr. Donald Macdonald seems to be a person in every way qualified for opening the eyes of an ignorant people to their real interests, both spiritual and temporal. His aspect and manner are firm and commanding, yet mixed with the greatest sweetness. Even when discoursing on the most common subjects, his style is animated, warm, and convincing. He is well versed in agriculture, and the management of different soils, which is of great importance in such a place; yet the people are so much prejudiced in favour of their ancient, uncouth modes, that but few follow his example. He is a Justice of the Peace, and is continually employed in distributing justice, for although the people are not much given to quarrelling or litigation, their rights in their farms are so confused and interwoven, that it is almost impossible to determine what share belongs to each. Supposing ten tenants possessing a farm, which is common enough, and every 'shot' or division of their arable land to consist of ten or more beds, or ridges, they do not take ridge about, and exchange yearly, nor yet part the produce, but every ridge is parted into as many subdivisions as there are tenants. Into tenths, twentieths, fourths, fifths, etc., every one managing and reaping his share, so that it would take a man to be master of fractions to be a tenant in Lewis. The pasture is regulated by the number of cattle, sheep, or horses, each possesses, and as there is no market for these save once a year, at the great tryste, some of the companies are often obliged to encroach on their neighbours' rights, or impose on their goodness. Thus it may well be supposed in what manner the ministers are harassed by continued applications for settling the most intricate differences.

There was a cause tried before Mr. Macdonald when I was there which lasted some hours, but it being conducted in Gaelic, I could only understand it by a general explanation. They submit, though sometimes reluctantly, to the decision of their pastor. From his court there are no appeals.

I am, sir, your ever faithful shepherd,

J. H.

DEAR SIR,—I took my leave of you at Barvas, near the Butt of the Lewis, where I arrived on the longest day of summer, and owing to the bright sky in the north, and the moon in the south,

beaming on the ocean, *there was no night there.*   Mr. Macdonald
and I made an excursion along the shores of the northern ocean.
The wind was indeed north-west, but the day was moderate, yet
there was such a tremendous sea breaking against the shore as I
never witnessed, nor indeed ever thought of before, there being
no land to break it nearer than North America or Greenland·
Every wave that came rolling against the perpendicular shore
burst into the air as white as snow, to the height of several
hundred feet.   There being no bays nor creeks on this coast
where any vessel can anchor, what a dreadful sight it must
present to mariners in a storm.

The sea having washed everything away but the solid rock, the
shore is in many places perforated by extensive caverns which
have never been explored.   In one place near to Europa Point,
or the Butt of the Lewis, of which we had a fine view, there is a
subterraneous cavern across the land from one sea to the other.
There is another in Uia which has been penetrated with lights to
a distance of nearly a quarter of a mile, and in which are annually
felled numbers of large seals.   We likewise saw several insulated
rocks along the shore, of considerable dimensions, and covered
with sea fowls which hatch on them.   Mr. Macdonald, who in
his walks seems to delight much in contemplating their natural
propensities, having little else here to attract his notice, described
several of their habits to me.   The Solan goose, great numbers of
which were continually passing and repassing, he described as the
most persevering and indefatigable creature in search of its

o

prey in the world, and adopting the most laborious means of obtaining it.   It does not hover and watch over any certain place, but flies straight on over seas and oceans until some chance fish attracts its notice, when it immediately springs up to a great height in the air, and as near as he could judge, always to about the same height, from which he supposed they saw most distinctly, and then, after a few moments' pause taking aim, it darts down into the sea with inconceivable rapidity and force ; and if it misses its prey, which must often happen, it again holds on its unwearied course.   He described a method of taking them used by some of the fishers, which if not so well authenticated might be looked upon as fabulous.   Well aware of the propensities of the Solan, they take a plank, in which they cut some apertures of a proper width.   These they fix along with their nets, and leave them swimming on the surface, having a herring or other clear fish fixed to each of the apertures on the lower side.   This catching the eye of the Solan goose, he, regardless of the intervening plank, dasheth his head into the hole, commonly with such force as to shatter his skull to pieces.

Mr. Mackenzie showed me a kind of sea-hawk, nearly as big as a Solan goose, the name of which in Gaelic signifies 'squeezer.' Whether properly applied, you may judge by the following description of its proceedings.   It is of so vitiated a taste that it seems to depend wholly for subsistence on the excrement of the Solan geese, and as it is only in a certain stage that it is of use for it, it takes the following method of procuring this singular

repast.   It fixes upon one goose which it pursues without inter-
mission, until it drops its excrement, which the squeezer hath the
art to snatch at before it reacheth the water, and well satisfied
with its alms, immediately quits that, and fixes upon another,
Those that we saw of them were always in pursuit of geese.

The other things that we saw worthy of remark were the hills
of sand contiguous to the manse.   These are an insurmountable
bar to improvement in that quarter, as a dry spring wind always
opens them, and lays the whole of the crops of grass or corn
adjacent, several feet deep in sand.   These hills are accumulating
from a sandy beach hard by, from which a strong north-west
wind fetcheth immense loads of sand.

On the top of one of these hills is situated St. Mary's chapel,
an ancient place of Popish worship.   It had formerly been on
the very summit of the eminence, but the sand is now heaped up
to such a height as to be on a level with the gables.   Yet the
eddying winds have still kept it nearly clear, so that it appears as
a building wholly sunk underground.   The baptismal font is still
standing in a place in the wall prepared for it.   There are many
of these in this parish, some of them of large and curious dimensions.   There are also on its coasts some of the most entire Nor-
wegian duns that are to be found in Scotland, the entrance to
which is from the top.   The purposes for which these were intended seem as much involved in obscurity as those of the
pyramids of Egypt, to which they bear some resemblance.   Mr.
Macdonald also showed me a hill of small size from which he had

seen sixty ploughs all going at a time. This will give you a very high idea of the fertility of the Lewis, or at least of the extent of the arable land there; and indeed this district of Ness, if it were not overstocked with people, and that it is under the most clumsy and untoward of all modes of cultivation, is certainly a *fertile place*, and is almost *wholly arable*, and composed of a variety of the richest soils, and what may seem remarkable, it enjoys the driest climate of the whole Western Highlands or Islands, as far as I could learn, even Islay not excepted.

This can only be accounted for by its lowness, there being no mountains of any height in the country.   It occupies the northeast corner of the island, and Mr. Macdonald assured me that though in summer the showers came over the Atlantic as black as pitch, they always parted before they came there, one part flying towards the mountains of Lochs and Harris, and the others to the hills of Sutherland; so that while the hay and kelp were rotting in these countries, the people on the north parts of Lewis were often getting theirs winnowed with ordinary expedition. Also that when he first settled there, on seeing the clouds gathering on the Atlantic (for an approaching rain is seen at a great distance on the open sea), he would make a great hurry in getting his hay or corn put into a way in which it would receive least harm, disregarding the old people, who told him that he needed not make such a fuss, for that 'none of yon would come near him.'   Of the truth of this he was by degrees agreeably convinced.

The frosts in winter are never intense, the snow sometimes covers the ground to a considerable depth, but never continues long, and in places where ground is covered with a proper thickness of herbage, the cattle thrive very well lying out on it all the winter.

When the wind blows from any of the eastern quarters, the weather is commonly mild and dry.   When from the western, hazy and accompanied with storms of wind and rain, and in the the late years of scarcity, when the failure of the crop on the most fertile countries of Britain left the inhabitants almost starving, these islands never had so plentiful crops, either by land or sea, the fishing being equally favourable; and as the value of the cattle rose, they never experienced better times.   But now, the case is for them sadly reversed; and whilst we are again swimming in plenty, they are perfectly reduced, by purchasing from other countries those necessaries of life which their own soil and bays have refused for the two last years to yield.

The people of this parish are industrious fishermen, and although their plans are the most simple, you will see by the papers that they always gain the most of the prizes held out by the society for dog-fish, cod, ling, and tusk.   They have a terrible sea to fish on, and as terrible a shore to land upon.   I could not avoid the old proverb, ' *Rather them as me.*'

Yours sincerely,

J.   H.

DEAR SIR,—Before I take my leave of Barvas it may not be improper to give you some idea of the mode of cultivation there, there being more arable land here than in any district of the Long Island, and a greater number of ploughs than in all the Long Island put together, for in this I reckon Ness included.

Their ploughs, numbers of which I saw, are very slender and shabby pieces of workmanship.   They consist of crooked trees selected for the purpose.   Through each of these a square hole is cut at the most crooked end, and here the stick that serves for the plough-head is fixed, and by wedging it above or below they give the plough more or less depth with great facility, as they give it less or more land by wedging it at the sides.   Then almost straight above the heel a small stilt is fixed, and this is the plough.   Although I saw several of their ploughs, not being there in the ploughing season, I have only seen two of them at work.   A greater curiosity can hardly be exhibited to one who is a stranger to their customs.   I could venture a wager that Cain himself had a more favourable method of tilling the ground. The man was walking by the side of the plough, and guiding it with his right hand.   With the left he carried a plough-pattle over his shoulder, which he frequently heaved in a threatening manner at such of the horses as lagged behind; but as it had the same effect on them all, and rather caused the most fiery ones to rush on, he was obliged sometimes to throw it at the lazy ones.   The coulter is very slender, points straight down, and is so placed that if it at all rip the ground it hath no effect in keeping the plough steady. The horses, impatient in their nature, go very fast, and the plough being so ticklish, the man is in a perpetual struggle, using every exertion to keep the plough in the ground, and after all, the furrow is in many places a mere scrape. The four ponies go all abreast, and such a long way before the plough, that at a little distance I could not imagine they had any connection with the man or it. They were all four tied to one pole, and a man, to whom the *puller* is a much more applicable name than the *driver*, keeps hold of it with both hands, and walking backwards as fast as he can, pulls them on. Those of them that walk too fast he claps the pole to their nose, which checks them. He finds means also to carry a small goad, with which he strikes the lazy ones on the face, asserting that that makes them spring forward. I had once an old brown mare, if he had struck her on the face he would have got her no farther in that direction. I can scarcely conceive a more disagreeable employment than that of this 'driver' as he is called. The ploughman's post being such a very troublesome one he is mostly in a bad humour, and if the line of horses angle, the plough in spite of his teeth is pulled out of the land to the side on which the line is advanced. This puts him into a rage, and he immediately throws the pattle, or a stone at the hindmost. Now, although the man may be a tolerable good archer, yet passion may make him miss, and the driver runs a risk of meeting with the fate of Goliath of Gath. But granting that this should never happen, and the ploughman's aim should always hold good, yet 'I own 'tis past

my comprehension' how a man can walk so fast the whole day
in a retrograde direction without falling, (when he must that
moment be trodden under foot by the horses). In fact I have
seen many people who would be often missing their feet on such
land although walking with their face foremost ; and it is a fact
that many of these drivers are hurt by accidents of the above
nature. Upon the whole, a more improper method of tillage cannot well be conceived, as much of the ground is missed, that of it
which is ploughed is rather crushed to one side than turned over,
and as two of the horses are obliged to go constantly on the
tilled land, it is by these means rendered full as firm as before it
was ploughed. You may perhaps think that I exaggerate in
calling the district of Ness at the Butt of the Lewis *fertile*, but I
am convinced that if the ground that I have had any concern
with had been tilled in the same manner, it would have produced
crops much inferior, if any at all.

The natives are very industrious in gathering manure, and
not inactive at making composts. They have one mode of
procuring manure, which is, I think, peculiar to themselves.
Their houses have very slender roofs, and are incapable of
carrying a layer of divot or turf below the thatch, like the
cottages in the south, but are merely covered with one light
layer of straw or stubble, for instead of reaping, they pull their
crops of barley wholly up by the roots, and those who are so
fond as to adopt the foolish modern custom of reaping, have
their stubble pulled up tightly after them. With this stuff the

houses are thatched anew at the commencement of every summer, having been previously stripped to the bare rafters, and
that which is taken off carefully spread upon the land about
the time when the crops begin to grow green.   This is
reckoned a valuable manure, and the land that it is spread
upon commonly produceth a good crop, but they complain
that it is a scourging one.   The method of spreading this
manure above is certainly injudicious, for being so well
sharpened by the soot and smoke, it might enrich the soil considerably if buried in, or incorporated with it.   But perhaps it
would not be convenient to strip their houses so early.

I am sure you are now thinking it is high time that I were
leaving Barvas. I beg your pardon, my dear sir, though I have
kept you a good while there; Malcolm and I were not long
there.   We left it early in the morning, stretching our course
towards Loch Roag on the west coast of Lewis. We wandered
on through trackless wastes, the whole of our course being
through swamps and deep morasses, whilst our journey was
constantly impeded by stagnant lakes, which, as the country
was so flat, never appeared until we were hard upon them,
casting us widely off our aim.   We were all the day uncertain
where we should land, but I felt much indifference, having
letters for the principal men of each district.   We saw a great
many sheep, goats, horses, and cattle, all straying at will on
the muirs ; and numbers of wild deer sprung from before us,
and fled with great swiftness towards Ben Barvas. At length,

P

growing hungry we sat down to eat some biscuit and cheese, which I told you before was as hard as wood. I now discovered that I had lost my pocket knife, and Malcolm had either lost his, or else he never had one; and in short, we found it impossible to get one bite of our cheese. Malcolm was despatched to a shealing, which was rather a covered cave, to borrow one. The inmates willingly sent the only one that they had, which was a piece of an old kelp-hook fixed in a deer's horn. This, instead of cutting our cheese, notwithstanding our utmost efforts, did not make the smallest impression. Malcolm was again despatched to a rivulet at a considerable distance, and came back carrying two large stones. On one of these we laid the cheese, Malcolm sitting on his knees held it with one hand and the knife with the other, d—ning them both most heartily; whilst I with the other stone struck with all my force on the back of the knife. By these rude means we at length got it hacked into irregular pieces, and having allayed our hunger, and thirst too, my dear Sir, we returned the knife, and proceeded on our journey. But here I must again take my leave for a few days, protesting that I am at all times,

Yours sincerely,

J. H.

www.ingramcontent.com/pod-product-compliance
Lightning Source LLC
Chambersburg PA
CBHW022140020726
47496CB00008B/2477